Duke of Havoc

Dukes of Destiny, Book One

Whitney Blake

Books from Dragonblade Publishing

Dangerous Lords Series by Maggi Andersen
The Baron's Betrothal
Seducing the Earl
The Viscount's Widowed Lady
Governess to the Duke's Heir

Also from Maggi Andersen
The Marquess Meets His Match

Knights of Honor Series by Alexa Aston
Word of Honor
Marked by Honor
Code of Honor
Journey to Honor
Heart of Honor
Bold in Honor
Love and Honor
Gift of Honor
Path to Honor
Return to Honor

The King's Cousins Series by Alexa Aston
The Pawn
The Heir
The Bastard

Beastly Lords Series by Sydney Jane Baily
Lord Despair
Lord Anguish

Dukes of Destiny Series by Whitney Blake
Duke of Havoc

Legends of Love Series by Avril Borthiry
The Wishing Well

Isolated Hearts
Sentinel

The Lost Lords Series by Chasity Bowlin
The Lost Lord of Castle Black
The Vanishing of Lord Vale
The Missing Marquess of Althorn
The Resurrection of Lady Ramsleigh
The Mystery of Miss Mason
The Awakening of Lord Ambrose

By Elizabeth Ellen Carter
Captive of the Corsairs, *Heart of the Corsairs Series*
Revenge of the Corsairs, *Heart of the Corsairs Series*
Shadow of the Corsairs, *Heart of the Corsairs Series*
Dark Heart
Live and Let Spy, *King's Rogues Series*

Knight Everlasting Series by Cassidy Cayman
Endearing
Enchanted
Evermore

Midnight Meetings Series by Gina Conkle
Meet a Rogue at Midnight, book 4

Second Chance Series by Jessica Jefferson
Second Chance Marquess

Imperial Season Series by Mary Lancaster
Vienna Waltz
Vienna Woods
Vienna Dawn

Blackhaven Brides Series by Mary Lancaster
The Wicked Baron
The Wicked Lady

The Wicked Rebel
The Wicked Husband
The Wicked Marquis
The Wicked Governess
The Wicked Spy
The Wicked Gypsy
The Wicked Wife

Unmarriageable Series by Mary Lancaster
The Deserted Heart
The Sinister Heart

Highland Loves Series by Melissa Limoges
My Reckless Love
My Steadfast Love
My Passionate Love

Clash of the Tartans Series by Anna Markland
Kilty Secrets
Kilted at the Altar
Kilty Pleasures

Queen of Thieves Series by Andy Peloquin
Child of the Night Guild
Thief of the Night Guild
Queen of the Night Guild

Dark Gardens Series by Meara Platt
Garden of Shadows
Garden of Light
Garden of Dragons
Garden of Destiny

Rulers of the Sky Series by Paula Quinn
Scorched
Ember
White Hot

About the Book

Lord Reeve Malliston, Third Duke of Nidderdale, is a brilliant military tactician with a musician's eccentricities. A favorite of the Duke of Wellington, he's called to fight on the fields of Salamanca. The English victory is supposed to be Reeve's defining accomplishment, but war is cruel to the duke, who is discharged from the battlefield nearly deaf and with two fingers missing. He comes home a disgraced and broken man, or so he believes.

After his lady wife dies under mysterious circumstances, nasty rumors abound that he went mad, that war shattered his mind and he murdered the mother of his two young daughters. With little care for the social consequences, he does nothing to combat the gossip and descends into debauchery, leaving his children under the dubious care of a pernicious governess and her sister, his equally uncivil housekeeper.

When yet another instance of domestic chaos greets him and his daughters beg him to intervene, Reeve suddenly decides to enlist his old comrade's daughter as their new governess. With this new woman to be both surrogate mother and tutor, Reeve plans on resuming his risqué lifestyle without worry or guilt.

But Miss Caroline Sedgwyck, though affectionate toward the children and levelheaded overall, is anything but docile. She sees right through Reeve's penchant for impropriety, much as he detects that her calm indifference to him is a facade. The two constantly test each other as Caroline challenges the duke to do what is best for his family, while Reeve stirs Caroline's passions.

Desire, friction, and friendship blossom in equal measure between them—is Caroline the woman to quell the *Duke of Havoc*? Will she restore the music to his soul?

Dedication

For Nick—who changed my mind about romance.

Acknowledgements

Enormous thanks to my editor, Scott Moreland, and to Kathryn Le Veque, who believed as much as I did that Reeve and Caroline had a story to tell.

Prologue

July 22, 1812
The Battle of Salamanca
Spain

I T HAD BEEN a glorious rout masterminded by the Duke of Wellington.

Now, it was the site of carnage. The fields of Salamanca, once shining waves of gold beneath the summer sky, were red with the blood of wounded men and horses that saturated the earth.

It had been a pristine place until 100,000 men found either their graves, or their victories. And living – however scathed or broken – counted as a victory.

Wellington had outsmarted the French. The man would be known as an offensive tactician from this battle forward because he'd exploited a weakness in what had been a solid defensive line. His decision had worked – the French were retreating, streams of their men fleeing the battlefield.

Ave omnes victors interemit.

All hail the victors.

For Reeve Malliston, Third Duke of Nidderdale, it was a day of diamonds. A commander in the British Heavy Cavalry Brigade, he came from an established line of soldiers and knights, and he looked upon his service under Wellington as a feather in his cap. He'd been personally requested by Wellington, who had been a friend of his deceased father.

He'd performed flawlessly under Wellington, sometimes despite dubious conditions, and he'd performed flawlessly today helping rout the French and protect British supply lines. Reeve was – or so he believed, anyway – a natural hero.

Truth be told, he was also something of a schemer and dreamer. He'd gone into the military to please his aged father – following in Papa's footsteps, as it were – but the truth was that Reeve had the soul of a poet, the heart of a musician, and the mind of a rogue that even the most severe discipline couldn't curtail. Even as a lad, he'd had a wild streak that his father had tried so hard to curb. Military school and fatherly beatings couldn't kill that spirit, and as a last-ditch effort, his father's old friend Wellington had taken Reeve under his wing.

Wellington understood him, oddly enough, and gave him assignments where Reeve's natural attributes would be best suited, like routing an entire flank of French troops. Reeve was innately cunning, and fearless, and his heroics had been successful.

The battle was dwindling. Reeve sat on the rise overlooking the battlefield as the smell of acrid gunpowder flared in his nostrils. The French were in petulant denial of their defeat, still persisting in firing off their nine-pounders in some areas.

Still trying to obliterate as many enemy soldiers as they can, poor bastards.

He'd moved his men out of range of the cannons and, even now, they were rounding up some of the French stragglers.

He was quite pleased with himself. Another victory, another fine mark upon his service record that proved to the world that he had some mettle in him. In the stories he would tell to his children in coming years, he would have undoubtedly single-handedly won this battle for the British.

And I will finally earn the respect that the dukedom title couldn't bring me –

Abruptly, Reeve's musing was interrupted.

Hot shrapnel carved into his flesh. He realized, somewhat aghast –

pain hadn't set in yet, only incomprehension – that a cannonball had just exploded several feet away from him. He glanced down to see a jagged line of ruby blood seeping through the new tear in his uniform, just along his collarbone. That wasn't the most shocking thing. He noted with strange detachment that his left hand was now missing its two middle fingers. The stumps were open, bloody messes.

Deciding he couldn't bear to see *that* any more, he looked around the field, at his lingering men that had been startled into action, into scurrying and sprinting away, some helping their wounded comrades into safer positions.

His last cogent thought was wry, steeped with a soldier's gallows humor. *Perhaps I didn't get us as well out of range as I assumed.*

Then, something – another shard, or just the sheer force of a new explosion – ruptured his left eardrum. Searing pain forced his mind to go blank.

Agony alone accompanied him into the dark.

Chapter One

November 1812
Yorkshire, England

*O*H, GOD...
  His head was killing him.

Reeve's head pounded so dreadfully that it was difficult to function on a fundamental level. He should have known better than to spend the entire night gambling and drinking but, evidently, he was a fool. Bracing himself, he stepped out of his phaeton into the offensive early morning sun, squinting because the light hurt his eyes. Squinting only worsened the anvil pounding in his head. The little blacksmith working away in his brain certainly was busy.

He'd just come home on a bright, cold morning after having been out all night.

Or was it two nights? Reeve wondered.

Christ, he couldn't remember. It was a race to get out of the sunlight and he took long, but comically halting, strides to the front door of his home – a pale-stoned beast of a building known as The Thornlands. His eyes were assaulted by the invasion of the sun; all he wanted was the succor of his fine bed or, perhaps, a soak in the tub first to ease his headache. Next time, he would know better than to accept a drinking challenge while at the gaming tables. Now, he was suffering for his rashness.

You dullard; you're old enough to know better. You're not some greenhorn.

Just as he reached the ornately carved oak panel that constituted his front door, it opened. His butler, the elderly but impeccably dressed Edgar, rushed at him. By the look on the butler's face, the duke knew that trouble lay in wait for him. Edgar's leathery-faced countenance was full of foreboding.

"What news brings you to me with such an expression?" Reeve asked, ready to get the matter dealt with, whatever it actually was, so that he could move on to solitude. "The ceiling of my home remains intact, I hope?"

Edgar rolled his eyes, giving the impression of one who wished to be anywhere else but where he was at the moment.

"My lord, the ladies are at it again," he said. He spoke in a pointedly loud voice when addressing his lord, as everyone in the household did these days.

If one didn't speak loudly, one simply wasn't heard. The damage to the duke's hearing those months ago on Salamanca had him almost completely deaf.

But Reeve heard him, clearly. He would have rather not heard him at all.

What a blasted surprise, he thought. "Ah," he said, resigned, his voice strained with hard-won patience. "The cats are in a bag, slashing at each other again. What's the trouble now? Has someone lost an eye?"

Edgar was genuinely distressed and did not approve of the sarcasm. "They have been nattering nonstop all morning. I fear, this time, that there truly will be a war."

Reeve had no time for hyperbole or dramatics, especially having served in an actual war. He was certain his head was about to bobble off his neck if he didn't get out of the sun.

"Tell me, Edgar, in precise terms, of the situation that has your nerves in tatters, and do let me indoors," he said as he tried to move into the shade of his stoop. "Be swift. I have no time for foolery."

Edgar tried to be succinct. "To my understanding," he said, "and you know how little of that is in supply in this house, Mrs. Humphrey decided to clean the children's room this morning. Meanwhile, Miss Ball had planned an etiquette lesson, but the children would have none of it – either the cleaning or the tutelage – so they locked themselves in their rooms and would not surface. Duckie tried to call them forth, but they ignored her, *then* she began fussing that their breakfast would go to waste."

Reeve gave him a droll expression. It was hard to manage snideness with such a headache, yet he did. "Say it is not so."

"It is true!" Edgar said, insistent. "But it grows worse, my lord. Duckie then demanded that Miss Ball and Mrs. Humphrey take responsibility for this great calamity and, of course, they refused. Now, all three women have taken up weapons. I fear for their safety, my lord, and 'tis a fine thing you have arrived home when you have. They need a battlefield commander, I fear."

Reeve looked at old Edgar as though the man had lost his mind. But as he thought on the situation, he could readily believe it. Although Edgar had a penchant for outrageous exaggerations, what he described was not outside the realm of possibility. The female members of his household were prone to useless squabbles. There had been some infamously ridiculous arguments.

Nothing had changed, even after he had been invalided. It was too much to hope for.

Exhaling a long-suffering breath, Reeve steeled himself, took the remaining steps to his front door and pushed it open.

He heard echoes of the fighting immediately as they rippled from the first of the double-parlors at the front of his home. An enormous, curving staircase was to his right, clinging to the wall. He knew that he could take the flight of stairs up to his room and none of the three women would be the wiser.

It was, perhaps, the best action to preserve his temper and his sanity, and one that would lessen the risk of exacerbating his headache. However, should they come to know of his evasion – and they would, because they always did – there would be no peace at The Thornlands. They would know their master had shirked his duties, as he'd shirked so many others since his return from the war.

It was, in fact, now his responsibility as the father of his children and lord of the house to settle any mishaps with regards to his daughters. But it was something he'd never had to handle until lately.

His wife's death had left him with greater responsibilities in terms of child rearing, ones he'd never considered undertaking. It had been their mother's lot to arbitrate these kinds of skirmishes.

Not that she ever really did.

Accompanied only by the greatest of displeasure and the blacksmith working away cheerfully in his head, Reeve headed for the parlor.

Although he *thought* he was prepared for anything, nothing could have prepared him for the sight that met him as he strolled into the room – not even Edgar's well-intentioned forewarning.

Behind him, Edgar had followed him inside. When he caught the expression on Reeve's face, he coughed discretely and uttered, "I told you so."

THE CARNAGE WAS spread wide for Reeve and Edgar to see: all three women brandished a weapon of attack.

First, Reeve glanced at the housekeeper. Mrs. Humphrey's bony fingers clutched a broom, and the way she pointed it at the cook, Duckie, suggested that she wanted nothing more than to sweep her away, permanently. To her right, Miss Ball, Mrs. Humphrey's sister and his children's governess, held a large book, possibly an atlas, over her head. It was a large, heavy object that would make a fierce projectile if launched.

Both women, looking almost skeletal in their ill-fitting morning dresses, had cornered the round and normally jolly cook.

Estelle "Duckie" Breem, who had been the family's cook for many years, seemed to be under threat of imminent attack. Both sisters looked sufficiently cross enough to do her substantial bodily harm. But the long pestle in Duckie's hands, held in a battle-ready pose, could easily serve as her saving grace against the sisters. More tellingly, the burning fierceness in her eyes gave no doubt as to her intentions in handling the pestle.

"If you witches think you can scare those poor children into submission like you done with their mother, then you don't know Duckie none!" she spat. Her accent was, and always had been, pure Spitalfields. "I ain't gonna allow that!"

"You old cow," said Mrs. Humphrey in a voice laden with disdain. Her own accent was pristine, without any drawn out vowels or dropped letters. "You will be gone from this house soon, mark my words. I have no idea what the duke sees in you or your cooking, but he will come to his senses soon. We will make certain of it!"

Miss Ball began nodding her head vigorously.

"We will," she hissed. "How dare you think to put yourself in opposition to us! You should pack your things this moment and never return!"

Reeve's eyebrows rose as he observed the scene. None of the women had taken note of his presence, which was surprising. A full-grown man had just entered their midst, but with the hatred filling the air, they seemed blind to all else. He'd seen furious rancor in them before, but not quite like this.

He'd seen enough.

"Ladies," he said. "Put down the weapons. Do it now."

Their reactions were instantaneous. The thud of Miss Ball's book, and Reeve observed that it was, indeed, an atlas – ironic considering

Miss Ball's knowledge of geography was nil – on the floor came first, followed by a loud yelp as the broom whirled about in Mrs. Humphrey's hands.

The bristly ends swished in Duckie's face.

Startled, the old cook released her hold on the pestle, which struck Miss Ball solidly on the foot. "Oh!" Duckie cried. "She hit me, she did! It hurts."

Miss Ball squeaked with pain, holding one leg and hopping on the other. Mrs. Humphrey rushed to her side, leaving poor Duckie nearly blinded.

Groaning in dismay, Edgar rushed toward Duckie to tender his help, even though all he ended up contributing to the fiasco was running squarely into her as she fumbled around with her hands over her eyes. They both fell in a heap. Meanwhile, the incensed sisters continued to screech loudly, raining condemnation on their adversary.

It was bedlam.

Sighing heavily, Reeve watched the madness, rolling his eyes at the sheer audacity of the situation and remaining well out of harm's way. He began to feel sorry for himself. All he'd wanted to do was go to bed and soothe his aching head. Truly, that was all he desired, and now he had havoc on his hands.

What did I do to deserve such a thing?

Without a doubt, he was too weary to listen to the nattering that was surely to follow when all three women wanted to tell their sides of the story. He always trusted Duckie more than the sisters. But such conversations were always inescapably nonsensical. Untangling the truth from the exaggerations, the tears, and the magnanimous elaborations had been his wife's responsibility.

But now that she was gone, it was yet another obligation she'd left to him, and it was merely one in a long queue of many. Reeve could do nothing more here. Nor did he want to. Without Lady Malliston around any longer, these foolish females would have to solve their own problems.

He simply didn't care.

The stairway in the foyer was calling to him and he answered, taking two steps at a time on the glossy surface until he reached the third floor. This was the children's level, where they slept and ate and had their lessons. It smelled of soap and powder, and of the flowers that his daughters liked to pick. There were little bits of green leaves scattered on the floor. His youngest liked to drag her bouquets along with her, and the clusters of dead leaves told him that the maids had not yet swept up after the morning's outing.

It was much more peaceful up here, away from the parlor's battle-field. It was almost welcoming, but Reeve had never felt fully welcome here. It held a host of sorrowful memories that all evoked the ghost of Lady Malliston, and not in a pleasant way.

She was a shadow that hung over the entire house like a sea fog that never lifted.

Coming to the great set of painted double-doors that marked his daughters' bedroom, he rapped softly. "Sophie? Phoebe? It is Papa," he said quietly. "Will you please open the door?"

The door flung open immediately.

"Papa!" his daughters said in unison as they threw themselves at him.

"Papa, where have you been?" asked Phoebe, her eyes huge.

It was a rush of love and affection, something he was highly un-comfortable with. Reeve could not comprehend his children's affection for him, and he certainly never did anything to encourage it. He was a failure at anything that had to do with fatherhood. It was a harsh admission to realize that what he felt toward Sophie and Phoebe was obligation, and this feeling had only grown since his return from the war.

He much preferred the gaming tables and clubs of York and London to any show of familial affection. And he had no inkling of what to say or do in response to the distress in his daughters' voices, or to the desperation with which they clutched his trousers.

Ill at ease, Reeve tugged his legs away from their clutches and looked down at their dark, curly heads and blue eyes. Only a year separated them in age, and they were the mirror image of one another, each possessing a round face and a small rosebud mouth. He was steeling himself for the day that they would be considered society beauties.

"What is this I have heard, Sophie?" he addressed his elder child, who was six years of age. "You and your sister refused to go downstairs?"

Sophie nodded fearfully, her lower lip trembling. She was a bright child, unafraid to voice her thoughts or opinions. "Miss Anna would have us paddled for eating dessert last night!"

Miss Anna Ball's self-discipline when it came to matters of enjoying food was legendary and, in fact, expanded past her own personal discipline to interfere with the children's.

As Sophie sniffled, Phoebe spoke up. "And this morning, Duckie took us outside and… and…" she said, the rest of her sentence lost to teary hiccups and garbled words.

Reeve wasn't unsympathetic, but shows of emotion only made his discomfort worse. "Speak up, little one," he said. "I must know what has happened."

But even if she did speak up, he couldn't exactly hear her. His younger daughter spoke in mumbled tones with a young child's heavy lisp. Her voice did not carry to his ears well enough, and Reeve detested speaking to her because of it – even though he knew it was truly no fault of the girl's.

Phoebe tried again. "We went… we went… outside with Duckie and… it… it rained last night…" she trailed off, and even if her life had depended on it, Reeve couldn't make out much other than "Duckie" and "rained". Phoebe's words came to him as many words did, muffled, as though they barely carried through cotton-and-beeswax he'd stuffed into his ears.

He attempted to draw it out of her again. "Phoebe, do you recall that Papa is hard of hearing?"

She went deeply pink and nodded.

"Do you recall why?"

"The war?" she asked uncertainly. Reeve only knew what she said because, although he could not read lips well, yet, he knew she would say "the war".

"Yes, that's right," said Reeve with a controlled tone.

"I'm sorry, Papa," said Phoebe.

"Thank you, my pet. Now, if you could please speak more loudly, I would appreciate it."

Phoebe simply burst into tears at that.

Sweet, quiet Phoebe was the fearful sort to begin with, which was made worse by Reeve's impatience in dealing with her. His frustration at being unable to hear her only came out as anger.

But Sophie, who always remembered their father was so very hard of hearing since his return home, had undertaken the duty of repeating her sister's words.

"Duckie took us for a lovely walk this morning," she said, more loudly than Phoebe could ever manage. "We picked flowers, and Mrs. Humphrey will have us whipped for bringing in mud because it rained last evening and had not dried up by dawn."

Reeve sighed. He knew that none of the women in the household would dare to paddle his children because he had made certain they wouldn't. However, his daughters were unaware of that directive. When they believed that they had done something wrong, they cowered in fear of their governess and the housekeeper. That nervousness was compounded by the fact that both women seemed to constantly, coldly threaten to use the paddle even though they knew they couldn't.

It was an idle threat that struck fear into Phoebe and Sophie's young hearts.

"That is ridiculous," Reeve said dismissively. "They will do nothing of the kind."

Unexpectedly, his words seemed to have the opposite effect with his girls, because their eyes welled with heavy tears. He fought down the urge to panic.

"But Miss Anna says so," Phoebe said. Her voice became higher. "She promises."

Their squeals and tears only made the pounding in his head worse. Reeve found himself consoling his children when he wanted to be resting his head. He tried to convince them that no one was going to spank them, but his pain just translated any well-meaning words into sharpness.

"I assure you that she will not spank you," he said. His voice was curt. "Papa is back, and there will be nobody taking a paddle to your backsides. Let this be the end of it."

Despite his brusque words, the girls finally seemed at ease. Satisfied, he quickly led the way into their nursery to ring for a maid. He wanted his girls tended so he didn't feel so guilty when he abandoned them to seek his bed. But Phoebe and Sophie, having not seen him in several days, began regaling him with the happenings in the manor since they'd last seen him.

Of course, rather than be even more churlish than he'd already been, he had to stand there and take it.

Reeve passed a hand over his eyes as he listened. Or at least pretended to listen. The truth was that he could only hear Sophie on occasion. She had a deeper voice than Phoebe, which helped, but she still lapsed into what would have passed for a more normal volume of voice, a lower volume, with any other adult. The ache in his head seemed to have increased tenfold since making his entry into his own house and, now, he was considering leaving it again just to find some peace.

Cool bed be damned to the Devil.

"Papa, will you stay home now, or will you be gone again so soon?" Sophie asked. Her gaze was beseeching.

Reeve heard *that* question. He looked at the pair, with those blue eyes that looked so much like their mother's. Maybe that was part of the problem: every time he looked at them, he saw Daisy, the cold blonde creature, fragile, but oh-so-wicked.

There was her ghost again, clinging to the house, poisoning his memories of his life since he'd married her. They were memories best forgotten, but that was difficult when he looked at his children. He couldn't think of Daisy in any terms other than evil, not after what she'd put him through after he'd returned from Salamanca.

He couldn't summon a shred of sympathy, not after what that she-wolf had done.

"Papa has businesses he must attend to," he said shortly. "You must allow Miss Anna to care for you."

Phoebe's lips started to tremble again. "But we don't like Miss Anna."

Reeve knew that, but he couldn't do anything about it today. "That is unfortunate," he said. "But Miss Anna is your governess, like it or not. She has great things of import to teach you, and you had better allow her to do what she is paid to do, or you will be sorely lacking in education. Is that what you want?"

But Reeve knew the girls didn't know what they wanted, or what might be best for them. Not really. They were still far too young. All they knew was their governess terrified them. They looked at each other, sadly.

"But we still don't want her, Papa," Sophie said, again. "She is wicked and cruel."

At a loss for what else to say, Reeve eyed his daughters. Phoebe had a finger stuck in her mouth, while Sophie had an arm thrown around her sister's small shoulders. Both were staring at him with earnest determination and hope.

Hope that, for once, he might listen to them.

Aspirations for a quiet bed or a healing bath were fading further and further. Reeve had come home entertaining hopes of hiding from the world, but his daughters had innocently thwarted his plans. Sophie, the more opinionated of the two, was a good sister. She took care of timid Phoebe well enough for Reeve not to worry about them. He knew that his daughters grieved the loss of their mother. But the sorry truth was that they had learned to get along without her well before she had died.

Yet the older they became, it was clearer that their self-sufficiency was waning. They needed, and wanted, their father's attention these days. But he couldn't bring himself to give it.

What in the world could make them so yearning?

What was he missing? The girls had a governess, a housekeeper, a cook, and several maids to tend to their whims and needs, so why did they still act as if they needed him?

Why wouldn't they leave him alone?

Thankfully, he was saved from further conversation by the maid's arrival. She swept in and whispered sweetly to the girls. They turned to her, diverting their attention from their father, and Reeve took the opportunity to quickly bolt for the door.

"The children must be hungry," he said to the maid – anything to keep them busy so that he could escape. "See that they are well fed. And send word to Mrs. Humphrey, Miss Ball, and Duckie to join me in my library in five minutes."

As the maid nodded and the little girls waved farewell to their father, Reeve quit the nursery, wondering if he was ever going to be able to tend to his throbbing head.

The Thornlands required too much of his attention today.

He had to do something about it.

Chapter Two

"I WILL NOT say it again, so listen well," Reeve said. His tone was a displeased growl. "Under no circumstances will any of you take a paddle to my daughters – nor will you ever threaten to do so. Is this in any way unclear?"

He spoke to a sullen group. Miss Ball went so far as to gasp with outrage as she glared at him in a mulish manner, but Reeve ignored the show of provocation. At least for now, he did. But there was a problem behind all of this, something he'd been ignoring since his wife's death.

It had been Lady Malliston who had brought Miss Ball and Mrs. Humphrey with her from her maiden home. From the start, they had only taken orders from Lady Malliston as if Reeve did not exist. He'd not been troubled by it. He didn't care how the house was run, or about anything else that he considered his wife's business, but now he was forced to assume her position without any of her authority.

Unfortunately, their old habits were deeply entrenched and neither Miss Ball nor Mrs. Humphrey saw any need to listen to, or otherwise obey, him. It was to be their downfall.

"By that same token," Reeve said, continuing under Miss Ball's murderous stare, "Under no circumstances will I *ever* come home to such an objectionable scene as I did today. It is detestable and unseemly, and no further debacle will be pardoned under my roof. It was shameful at the very least and a terrible example to my children.

Do you understand this?"

The ladies grew quiet at the admonition, with Miss Ball and Mrs. Humphrey passing rebellious glances. Duckie, however, was more serene and receptive; she'd been with the Malliston household since Reeve was a child and, much like the duke's two young daughters, she detested the sisters. They'd been nothing but trouble since Lady Malliston had brought them in, and she had always been the odd man out.

"I shall abide by your words, my lord," Duckie said. She set her jaw. "But if threatened, I should be allowed to defend myself."

Reeve looked at the woman. Estelle Breem was, by nature, an inoffensive, well-meaning, and easy-going creature. These were the very reasons that Reeve thought of her with reasonably warm regard. However, the two sisters seemed to draw out a combative nature that had been hidden within her. If Reeve didn't show more care, the three women would degrade his home into a battleground. They were growing increasingly disgruntled by sharing responsibilities over a household that no longer included Lady Malliston.

In more accurate terms, the sisters were disgruntled by Duckie's presence. They had been trying to oust her since their arrival, and their efforts had only intensified since his wife's passing.

Reeve knew all of this. Because he would rather keep his sanity as well as his word, he had given all three, regardless of who was in the right or wrong, a dressing-down which he hoped would put a firm end to their unreasonable, destructive disagreements. Duckie had acknowledged his directive, but the two sisters had yet to respond. He wasn't surprised; they were a disagreeable lot. But he wasn't going to let them ignore him.

"I will have your agreement on the matter, Miss Ball and Mrs. Humphrey," Reeve said, his irritation clear in his voice. "Is this understood?"

The women didn't answer right away, making it obvious they had little respect for him. Therein lay the problem: they'd never had any respect for him. The only person they'd showed any regard for had taken her own life four months ago upon her husband's return from the war.

That only further exacerbated an already melancholy issue. They put the blame squarely upon Reeve for Lady Malliston's suicide.

They'd even spread rumors that he was to blame. He knew they had.

Therefore, showing the duke the esteem he was due was something of a struggle for them.

But, thought Reeve with perverse satisfaction, *they have little choice.*

If they wanted a roof over their heads and some position of respect, then the abject resentment they held for him would have to be cast aside at some point. He would settle for less antagonism, even if he couldn't get true respect. Neither old woman wanted to be thrown out into the streets. After several moments, it was their pragmatism that won.

"We would not dare to displease you, my lord," Mrs. Humphrey finally said. She looked away from him as she added, under her breath, "At least not within your hearing, which leaves us plenty of room to conduct ourselves how we wish."

Reeve could not hear her at all, which in and of itself left him furious. But it was Duckie's deeply offended scowl that told him Mrs. Humphrey had mumbled something unsavory about *him.*

He shook his head slightly at the cook, though he appreciated her loyalty.

"Would you care to repeat yourself, Mrs. Humphrey?" he asked her. "I thought I had made myself quite plain, but if you are having trouble understanding my wishes, I am happy to repeat what I expect of you."

"No, my lord, I do not care to repeat myself and I require no further explanations."

Reeve leveled her with a cool glare. He took a breath, about to speak again, but she muttered, "Little wonder my lady couldn't bear such a husband. You are hardly a whole man, are you?"

Again, he couldn't hear her words, only the viperous tone with which she murmured them, but dear Duckie appeared ready to launch herself at Mrs. Humphrey.

"How frightfully rude you are, Mrs. Humphrey," spat Duckie. "*And* unkind—"

Reeve brought up a hand to stay the women, who were clearly itching for more confrontation.

It was the wrong hand. Unfortunately, he had always been rather ambidextrous before suffering his injuries and, in conversation as well as daily life, he'd often used his left as much as his right. It was a hard habit to break.

Miss Ball pounced on the opportunity to insult him further and said in a soft, malicious way, "No, Sister, he is hardly whole, is he?"

Reeve would have liked to have given both women a sound verbal lashing – had he the energy for it – but he didn't. Wishing to avert a continued crisis, he said crisply, "You know as well as I, Miss Ball, that I have no idea what you have just said. However, I understand what you are doing. While you may do so at your leisure and behind closed doors, you will not subject me to your petty barbs when I have better things to do. This discussion is about my children."

These two were taxing what was left of his already compromised patience.

"Please give me your word, such as it is, that neither of you will lift a finger against either Phoebe or Sophie. It is strictly out of the question."

He barely waited for the sisters to nod crisply, reluctantly, and dismissed them with another imperious wave of his hand. This time, he purposefully used the ruined one. He refused to feel shame just because these harpies wished him to feel inferior.

Before Duckie reached the door, she turned and gave him an apologetic look. He did not smile, but he inclined his head in thanks.

Even after they were gone, he continued to stand where they had left him, pondering the situation he found himself in. It could not continue unchecked. Looking around his lavish library, which smelled of old leather and mellow tobacco, he should have found comfort in the familial surroundings. It had been his father's library, and his father's before him. But Reeve found no comfort. All he could think of was the havoc of this place. Chaos and bad fortune had stalked him like a hunter for the last four months. He was tired to the bone of it.

But the two sisters his wife had brought with her to The Thornlands caused so much of the trouble. If only he could dismiss them and employ others in their stead. As much as he wished he could, it simply wasn't feasible. They had nowhere to go, it would cause even more upheaval for his daughters, and – this was far less of a priority, if he was being as honest with himself as he ought to be – Lady Malliston had once made him promise to keep them at the manor.

Although she was gone, Reeve found the idea of going back on his word repulsive, not because he still cultivated any love for Daisy, but because he knew people would talk.

Bitterly, he thought, *They already speak so ill of you… remember?*

Reeve felt obliged to retain the women in his household unless they would go voluntarily. That was as likely to happen as his hearing healing itself. And as a result, he would continue to suffer their petty agendas and squabbles.

There was so much more to everything than the whispered rumors and deep misconceptions. Still, they dominated Reeve's life. There wasn't a person in the entirety of York or the whole of England, probably, who did not think they knew Reeve's honorable reputation had ended with his service in the war.

The *bon ton* that had once embraced him now refused to accept him. He used to be considered handsome, gregarious, and a pleasure to have at any ball or gathering. Before he'd married, he was one of the most eligible and badgered bachelors.

In spite of everything he'd been before, he'd returned from the battlefield a man in turmoil. He could neither navigate his mind, nor his newfound disabilities.

From the *ton's* perspective, his darling wife had only killed herself as a result of his black moods, his inability to make peace with himself.

She was hardly to blame, people said, when she lacked a sane, hardy husband.

That's what was largely believed. Although it was painful to do so, Reeve could admit that, perhaps, he was responsible for some of that opinion. He had come home in the middle of what should have been his most defining victory. His term of service was finished for him by irrevocable injury.

Then his wife died by suicide scarcely a month after his return. The gossipmongers had run absolutely mad with it and, back then, he hadn't cared enough to change their minds.

If he wasn't feeling as though he was containing a tempest within his very skull, he felt numb, encased by ice. He couldn't explain it to anyone, whether surgeon or layman. None of them knew what it was like to be whole, to have your dreams within your reach, then to have it all compromised.

It wasn't just Lady Malliston's ghost that lingered within The Thornlands: the phantom of his ruined reputation, fueled by the fervent belief of the *ton* who spoke so eagerly of his troubles, lurked around every corner.

Daisy's death had been a shocking event. But in keeping with the public's voracious appetite for sensational events, they fell over one another not to understand, but instead to discuss and relish the matter.

Suicide was always worthy of inspection, and tongues wagged at a steady pace, all thanks to fodder provided by the opportunistic and malicious sisters, Miss Ball and Mrs. Humphrey.

Without their interference, things could have settled to a calmer state.

It might have taken time; it might have taken months or years.

But Reeve might not be in such dismal circumstances now.

He had known all of this at the time, but he hadn't cared. His mind, which was as shattered as his hearing, simply wouldn't allow for it. He sealed his own fate by doing the unforgivable: he held himself aloof, sequestered in his manor house, depriving people of more fuel for the gossip they sought with their self-serving invitations and calls to visit him in the loss of his wife.

He had ignored them.

Quickly enough, they tired of waiting for him. So they told the story however they deemed fit, with as many differing embellishments as there were colors of paint. Reeve could well imagine that his former peers, but especially anybody who was beneath his own station, like Miss Ball and Mrs. Humphrey, found great satisfaction in spreading tales of his madness.

He was certain his social equals spoke of how the war drove him mad, so irredeemably mad that his lady wife killed herself simply to end the torment of being subjected to it, and how he now lived a life of debauchery.

To them, he was a killer. At least the murmurings about his lascivious tastes were true.

But all of that condemnation eventually bred fear, which was, in its way, useful.

There were not many who would venture to cross him when it came to matters of politics. He was richer than most and everyone knew he had the ear of the Duke of Wellington.

And they further knew better than to seek trouble from the *Duke of Havoc*. Reeve supposed his detractors did not realize he knew the derogatory sobriquet they'd given him.

Everything he touched, it was said, became mired in madness.

But back when I should have been airing the truth, I was barely retaining my sanity, he thought.

Lost in his dark remembrances, Reeve left the library, finally in search of his bed. There would be no time for him to bathe now. Making his way to his chamber, he slunk into the room and closed its heavy velvet drapes, shutting out the glaring winter sunlight that filtered through the windows.

As he fell into bed at last, a possible solution occurred to him.

Heavens above, he wanted sleep. But his thoughts lingered on his children. Sophie had insisted that she and her sister did not like Miss Ball. Reeve had to admit that she was a cruel feline of a woman. He had never liked her and could not blame his daughters for how they felt.

If he couldn't get rid of her... perhaps he might have peace if someone else took the position as a tutor and governess for his girls.

It was Miss Ball they feared most, when all was said and done.

He could give her other duties, far away from Phoebe and Sophie, and far away from him. Perhaps what the girls really needed was a new face, someone who wasn't connected to the terrifying thought of a paddling. Perhaps a new tutor could change the dynamics of the household enough for Reeve to be left alone.

On the wings of that particular idea came another thought, which proposed an outlandish, yet ideal, if he could arrange it, solution to his predicament.

Reeve had realized what he could try.

A friend from his battlefield days, a mild-mannered music teacher who'd been called to serve under him, had spoken very highly of his daughter's quick mind. It might be difficult to convince her to come to The Thornlands, given Reeve's reputation. Impossible, even.

You do not have anything to lose in trying, though.

With a grumble, Reeve rolled out of bed, clothes rumpled, hair mussed, head still pounding, and reluctantly returned to his library. No matter how much he wanted to, he couldn't quite rest while a potential resolution was in sight. Anyway, closing his eyes did nothing to abate his headache.

Besides, there was a gaming tryst tonight at his friend's hunting cottage just outside town, and Jonathan Polk, Earl of Flemminghall, often threw the best parties. They were really just an excuse for nights of gaming and decadence. Reeve knew he had to be somewhat rested if he was to attend.

And he certainly did not wish to remain here on the coattails of such a spectacular spat in his parlor. While he trusted Duckie, he suspected that Mrs. Humphrey and Miss Ball would not be contrite enough to hold the peace. Therefore, it was best to get household matters out of the way if he wanted to leave Sophie and Phoebe for another night without feeling guiltier than he already did at the prospect.

It could be several nights, he reminded himself.

Reeve sat heavily at his desk in his favorite armchair. Pulling forth paper from a lacquered box, he began to write a missive in his surprisingly beautiful handwriting. It was the one thing his father had praised about his schooling. Somehow, along the path to adulthood, Reeve had perfected exquisite penmanship. He had also mastered a way with words that told the complete truth, but couched it in more desirable terms than the actual reality did. He described his daughters as "most charming" when, truly, he had met few other children to compare them to and they grated on him. But he reasoned that, in their own unique ways, Phoebe and Sophie could be quite ingratiating. At the very least, they were well behaved.

The more he wrote, the more hope he possessed in this tenuous plan.

Already, he could imagine his household becoming more peaceful.

There was still the lingering question of how it would really come to pass, but he squirrelled it to the back of his mind.

When Reeve sought his bed again, it was only after the missive was properly bound to be sent out early in the morning. He cautiously congratulated himself; he didn't know why he hadn't thought of it before. His daughters simply needed a new governess. A warmer, kinder woman to look after them. He was reasonably confident that if it could be arranged, this solution would finally allow him a respite from the household madness.

With some luck, this will change things at The Thornlands, he thought.

Chapter Three

Dear Arthur,

I trust that you have been well.

I fear that you have forgotten all about me now that you are home. I, on the other hand, still remember your camaraderie during those dark days. Remember the night when we both had to journey on foot to the village just for a bottle of ale? My memory dwells upon that night in particular. You told me of your daughter, of whom you were very proud, and you declared her the one reason you would not die in battle. You so fondly recounted that her knowledge covered a wide array of topics and would put many a man to shame – this has rendered her the perfect candidate for my purpose.

I am in need of a tutor for my two daughters. You must have heard about the death of my lady wife shortly after I returned home. Given the state of my return, and following such a deep loss, my daughters need feminine guidance in their educations. Barring the possibility that your daughter may already be married – for my own selfish reasons, I hope that this is not the case – would she be willing to come to The Thornlands in my employ as a tutor for my daughters? Sophie is six, while Phoebe is only just five – both are the most charming children. I daresay that coaching them would be a delight for your clever daughter.

I am willing to offer her a handsome sum per year for her services, half of which I will have sent to you upon her arrival at The Thornlands should you agree to my terms. I am also willing to meet *any conditions you might have – if, of course, they are reasonable.*

If you are in agreement, you must send me a response immediately, stating your approval and hers alongside your conditions, if any. I would prefer your daughter begin her duties as soon as possible.

I shall await word from you.

Your friend,
Reeve Malliston

For the second time, Caroline Sedgwyck read the letter, which was stamped with the Duke of Nidderdale's seal, and her eyes scanned the page with interest.

"Oh, Papa," she said. "This is a stroke of good fortune."

Arthur Sedgwyck sat across the table from his daughter as the morning sun streamed through dirty windows into their little dining room. The papered walls were peeling in the corners, and the sadly scuffed furniture had seen better days. Everything, in fact, had seen better days, including both Caroline and Arthur's attire.

But the old man beamed with joy as his daughter spoke, as though they were wearing and surrounded by the greatest of fineries.

"Indeed, it is," he said. "It could be an answer to prayer."

Arthur was a quiet man of few words, but Caroline had learned to understand the meanings and emotions behind what little he said. Further, she knew that this letter from his former comrade-in-arms could well be the answer to their troubles.

Even if that old comrade was the infamous Duke of Nidderdale.

The *Duke of Havoc*, she thought. They'd heard the rumors. Everyone had.

But Caroline was in possession of more practicality than fancifulness and it was not in her nature to believe gossip or hearsay. Amongst her small but intimate group of friends, she was always the voice of reason when one became too carried away by fantasy or disgruntlement.

There was much-needed money involved here and she was in no

position to allow either fear or potential untruths to rule her head.

A music teacher living in York with his only daughter, Arthur had possessed the easiest of dispositions and sunniest of smiles before the war. He had been solidly positioned within the middle of York society, respectably viewed in the same way as a favored merchant or tailor or modiste. The Sedgwycks lived comfortably, if not lavishly. As a child, Caroline lacked for nothing and their house was clean and warm. It was full of books, Arthur's musical instruments, and even some paintings. They did not have servants who lived with them, but they had one maid. If anything needed to be fixed or mended, it did not cause dismay or panic.

But then Arthur had heeded the call of battle and gone to fight around Arapiles.

The little teacher had come back a changed man; the light in his eyes was gone and the song in his voice was all but silenced. He'd resumed his old occupation only for the sake of survival, without any true gusto.

Caroline was the first to admit that his music, his soul, had been tainted by the war, even though the English claimed victory.

For her father and, she suspected, the *Duke of Havoc – the Duke of Nidderdale*, she mentally corrected herself – the victory was, indeed, a hollow one. Arthur still would not speak in detail about his service. Only time would tell if he ever would.

Now, the situation was quite dire for the Sedgwycks.

These days, members of the *ton* preferred to send their children or wards off to expensive schools or to stay in the City where they could be taught a variety of topics, including music. Arthur's few patrons consisted of those who could not afford such educations. As such, he earned very little. While he was always kind to Caroline and had, at first, endeavored to obscure the extent of their circumstances, that they were close to sinking into debt, she was intelligent and could not mistake the deteriorating house for a sign of his professional and financial success.

After many evenings of cajoling her father into telling her the truth, Caroline finally knew what the thin scrapes of butter upon their toast, the dwindling household items – sold, as it transpired, to attempt to meet some of their expenses – and her threadbare dresses all signified.

Living on little means did not frighten her, but the consequences of becoming a debtor did.

The Duke of Nidderdale's unexpected letter felt unreal. As a girl, Caroline had never quite believed that her education, insisted upon by her mother long before her death in childbirth, then faithfully carried out by her father, would matter in a material way.

Now, she had the opportunity to put it all to use. While she'd always appreciated being so well read, a rarity in many girls and women, she never knew exactly what use it might serve.

Husbands, for example, did not generally wish for wives who could talk circles around them in conversation or knew as much about political affairs as they did. Caroline was not particularly bubbly or gregarious, but she was not afraid of having her own views.

Perhaps Lord Malliston wasn't a desirable employer, but that couldn't be helped.

I shall have to take what I can get, thought Caroline.

"The duke thinks highly of you," she said after a moment. "He seems kind. His words are thoughtful."

Arthur took the missive back from her when she offered it. His light hazel eyes skimmed the graceful penmanship.

"I think highly of him," he said. "Reeve… Lord Malliston… was a fine man when I knew him. He even told me to disregard the use of his title, although I would never do so now. The battlefield does strange things to men, but I cannot say that all of them are bad."

His words contradicted the slight unease she read in his careworn face. He had read the letter first, alone in his dreary little study, and then called her into the dining room so that she could read it, too. Since that moment, Caroline had sensed an uncharacteristic disquiet, an underlying hum of anxiety that she only associated with her father's manner when she was roused from her own sleep by the sound of his shouting.

He had terrible nightmares of things he would never divulge to her, no matter how much she begged.

When she succeeded in waking him, he often possessed the same air of uneasiness that he had now.

Arthur had only mentioned Lord Malliston once or twice and, in those cases, had never related very much about him.

Most of what Caroline had heard had been the rumors that milled through York and its surrounding towns like unruly stray dogs. What she'd heard about the duke did not flatter him. She did not necessarily believe any of it, though, and would not until the rumors were proved true. If they were true.

"He will offer a very generous amount for a tutor. I am certain," she said, attempting to draw out a more telling comment from her father, who seemed to be mired in thought. "Don't you think?"

Arthur nodded at last. "He appears to be in quite a haste to find a tutor for his girls," he said. "His wife died most suddenly. Although they are still very young, I imagine their children's education must have suffered drastically amidst all that upheaval."

Caroline shook her head with pity. "It is such a sad thing about Lady Malliston," she said. "Those poor children, losing their mother at such a young age."

That, at least, I can understand well, she thought.

She was finding it difficult not to think about her potential charges more than her potential employer. She had lost her mother at birth. While she never knew her affections, her father's praise and love for his late wife gave Caroline a clear sense of who she had been. Arthur exalted Lily Sedgwyck to the heavens and her portrait still hung against the wall in the drawing room.

It was almost, fancied Caroline, a reverent shrine. The portrait was treated as an image of a long dead saint or an ethereal angel. Arthur could never bring himself to move it, just as he could not bring himself to sell all of Lily's old possessions. Caroline had been given several, though none were terribly costly. Among them were a comb and a rosy silk ribbon that had faded with age.

Many times, Caroline had faced that portrait, believing, hoping, that her mother watched over her and that the painting really was an icon. It captured Lily's warm smile and, somehow, the painter had conveyed wisdom and kindness through her green eyes. Many swore they were exactly like Caroline's, and she was proud of the association. Proud that it tied her to a mother she had never known, a woman her father never quite seemed to stop grieving.

As a widower, he could have remarried but never had. This wasn't lost on Caroline, who was no great romantic but acknowledged how fortunate her parents had been in their love. Her father's loss was tragic.

Despite the fact that Lord Malliston himself inspired such loathing and scorn, Caroline found herself drawn to his daughters' predicament.

I just need to know a little more about the truth behind these rumors.

Thinking quickly, Caroline decided it would be best to gently coax her father into saying more about his old commanding officer. "What might you say about the duke's manners and disposition, Father?" Caroline asked. She hoped it would prompt him to speak his mind on both the man and his offer. "Would you say he would be easy to live with and work for? If I go to his home, I shall be spending a great deal of time there."

But Arthur remained silent following her query. Even before going to battle, he chose his words carefully and would never speak ill of another man. He was deliberate and thoughtful in everything he did.

Now, he was almost taciturn.

Although he must have known Caroline was taken with this offer, she could see that he had some reservations.

Come on, Father.

He finally ventured, "Regarding his manners and disposition to those in his employ, you will have to discover that for yourself. My estimation of the man originates from our time in battle. If you would like to know what I learned from that, I found him upstanding, agile, sound of mind, and, despite what others who knew him might have contended, unassuming. I think his natural gregariousness was read as some kind of arrogance. And he was a great favorite of the Duke of Wellington himself. That inspired some spite."

This was the first time her father had truly mentioned anything specific about his own service. Granted, it was about another soldier, an officer, but that alone marked something significant about the duke. She conjectured that he must have made a good impression upon her father.

Would it not have been insensitive, she might have pointed this out to him.

Best not, she thought. *I don't want to embarrass him.*

Perhaps the nasty, pernicious gossip had not tarnished her father's opinion of him. This hope, paired with what was for Arthur, high praise, made Caroline confident that she would soon be packing her trunk and reticule for Easingwold to begin the new position. Truly, she had no objection to putting her education to such use, especially given the potential of financial help to her father, and that was the greatest lure of all.

But her eagerness was dampened at the thought of leaving her father alone in the house. Well, not entirely alone... his widowed younger sister, Aunt Lydia, would be there to tend to his needs. She had stayed with Caroline while Arthur was away fighting, and had never quite managed to find her way home after his tour had concluded. This was not wholly unacceptable because Aunt Lydia brought with her a widow's pension. She was not a drain on their already stretched resources.

She, a woman shaped vaguely like a mantis, Caroline had to note, was a little bossy and definitely flighty, but she was a good, true soul. She adored her brother and loved Caroline dearly.

Aunt Lydia will at least be some company for him.

It seemed like a sound plan. In that moment, Caroline saw no reason why she should not accept the position. Arthur put the letter on the table. Again, Caroline picked it up and studied it, her eyes deliberately pausing over each word in a final bid to find any implicit shortcomings in the offer. Finding nothing objectionable, she mused on his address and title.

The Thornlands – a fearsome name for a place that supposedly hid a fearsome crime. Caroline swallowed. There was no use in avoiding the inevitable. She needed to clarify something.

"Father," she said. "I must ask you…" she trailed off.

"What is it?"

"We have danced around it. This *is* the same man alleged to have killed his wife, is it not?"

Arthur sighed, stood up from the dining table, and went into the parlor, where he landed upon a worn leather chair facing the hearth. Caroline followed him to the low flames; she understood this was not his avoidance or a dismissal. He was more prone to the chill at his age, even during daylight hours.

The old chair moved closer to the flames by the day, it seemed.

He moved the chair even closer now as he pondered his daughter's question. Unspoken, it had been hanging between them like a menacing noose.

Now that I've voiced it, he cannot ignore it, thought Caroline with grim satisfaction. *Or pretend we haven't* both *heard the claims.*

"You know that as well as I do. Do not be coy," he said as he settled back in his chair. "What would you have me say?"

Caroline moved to sit on a little stool by the hearth, her back against one of the chair's armrests. "You have not mentioned it at all."

"Must I?"

She sighed, annoyed, but trying not to show her impatience. "Are you saying that the rumors do not matter to you?" she asked. "I seek your thoughts on the matter of the *Duke of Havoc*." She deliberately used the abrasive, disrespectful nickname. "Please tell me."

A smile played on his pale lips as he looked down at her. "Dear Caroline, you must know that an old man like me has to gather his thoughts before spitting out his words."

He was toying with her; she could see it. *Now is no time for sarcasm.*

"We have never discussed this… but now we must," she persisted. "They say the battlefield turned him mad. I am not certain I believe this, unless I am only to believe it drove him to the same blackness of mood as you. Could he have murdered his wife in their very own home? Leaving his children to fend for themselves without a mother and a murderous father?"

She stared into her father's face, searching for his honest answer.

Arthur shook his head and pinched the bridge of his nose with his right thumb and index finger. His brows knit together in consternation.

I have pushed him too far, thought Caroline.

She rarely, if ever, mentioned his nightmares, the chronic sullen silences, the strange sheen his eyes sometimes gained when he gazed into the fire – or at nothing but the peeling wallpaper, which was more unnerving – but they both knew he was susceptible to the darkness that his music, even as faded as it was now, kept at bay.

Aunt Lydia, who was not as quick as Caroline, had never noticed.

But if the duke was mad in the same manner that her father was mad, Caroline was not frightened.

"Do not repeat such morbid things," said Arthur curtly. "Only small minds latch on to them. I do not believe the tales. I suggest that you discard them, too."

So that was his opinion. Caroline thought as much, but she had needed to hear it from him directly. "As always, I value your thoughts," she said, worrying her lip gently with her teeth. "But there can be no smoke without fire, as you often say."

"Yes," Arthur said, with surprising sharpness. Caroline's eyebrows rose. "But it is nobody's business to stoke the fire of another person's misery. Lord Reeve Malliston was a good man when I knew him. That is all I care to know. I do not believe him capable of murder or cruelty…"

Unless it's on a battlefield, thought Caroline.

"Therefore, I will leave the decision with you, as well as the freedom to reply as you please. Know that whatever you decide shall bring no argument from me."

Mutely, Caroline nodded.

"How his lady wife died, I cannot say. But I do not think the duke is responsible for her passing." Arthur brought his hand to the top of Caroline's head, stroking it as though she was still a girl and not a woman of one and twenty. He was so gentle that his fingers barely caught on her dark red curls.

"Very well. I did not think he was, either. There must be more to it than the vile stories, must there not?" she said, smiling weakly.

"Yes, my girl. Now, if you'll pardon me, I must ready some exercises for a pupil. Our unexpected letter has rather interrupted my routines."

Arthur stood from his old chair and quit the room, leaving Caroline sitting in thoughtful silence.

Caroline was pensive, but she was certain of one thing. For a man to be championed by her father was indicative of his true character.

Not gossip.

Still, the fact remained that her father provided one caveat: all he knew about Lord Malliston came from their time shared within a war. He knew nothing of the man after his return. There was such a great disparity between what Arthur said and what the public keenly whispered. It caused concern, even for a creature so practical as her.

She and her father badly needed the stability this position could offer. But it was equally true that to accept that position at The Thornlands could, in time, subject her family to the same gossip that plagued the Duke of Nidderdale.

That would ruin what's left of Father's business, a sneaking, traitorous voice said in her mind. *Not to mention any of my own prospects.*

Were she in a less serious mood, she might have chortled at the thought. She was next to penniless. She was not of the *ton*. She had no prospects to speak of. Such things were for other women with lives that were leagues away from hers.

She did not mind being a spinster if that was to be her fate after all, but she could not be a poor one.

And she would not let her father suffer if she could enter employment that could better them.

It remained that Arthur felt there was nothing wrong with Lord Malliston, and he also respected Caroline's autonomy in nearly all matters. He was an unconventional father and it was why he'd left the final decision in her hands. She trusted him, and he would never knowingly allow her to put herself in peril. This proposed situation, by his measure, was neither perilous nor ridiculous.

Perhaps the money will outweigh any ill effects my association with The Thornlands might bring to our reputations.

Indeed, she decided, she had to be brave enough to take the chance.

Eyes shining with determination, Caroline stood and proceeded to the writing table in her father's study. So that there would be no confusion between parties, and so that the duke would understand that this was a binding agreement, she put pen to paper, carefully writing out her terms.

Yes, she would accept the position and, yes, his payment was acceptable.

Chapter Four

Three Weeks Later

REEVE WAS IN the best of spirits as he awaited the arrival of his girls' new tutor. Over a fortnight had passed since the idea struck him with the force of a hammer's blow – notable even amidst the pounding in his head – and it was still hard to believe it was coming to fruition.

Today, he had instructed that Sophie and Phoebe both be dressed in their finest attire. He even spent close to three solid minutes in their company to explain to them what was about to happen. Miraculously, neither of his daughters managed to irk him. They looked very presentable. Phoebe was in her favorite color, a forest green, and Sophie wore a blue frock that matched her eyes.

"You will find her most agreeable," he had promised. "*Much* more agreeable than Miss Anna."

They'd exchanged two blue-eyed looks that he thought were laced with skepticism. Given their tender ages, he wasn't sure if they were capable of such an emotion but, then again, given his behavior toward them in the past, perhaps they were coming to learn that their papa wasn't always altogether present or sincere when he addressed them.

Neither girl had voiced her enthusiasm, but neither had complained. He took that as a good sign, inwardly praised God for the good fortune of *no hysterics*, and proceeded to inform them of exactly how he wanted them to behave in Miss Sedgwyck's presence. They were to be polite and speak only when spoken to.

Reeve ruefully acknowledged, at least to himself, that he had exaggerated his daughters' praises in his letter to Arthur. In his own defense, they were not troublesome girls, and he was not covering up any spoiled or uncouth habits to lure in the new tutor.

He just didn't know them as well as he ought to, but what was there to know about little girls?

And I can barely tolerate Miss Ball and Mrs. Humphrey when I see them, myself. I cannot blame either Phoebe or Sophie for their aversion to the bitches.

He nursed hopes that with a new woman, particularly one as young as Arthur's daughter, in the house to tutor the girls there would be fewer dramatic spectacles and more stability. In theory, Phoebe and Sophie would be better occupied with a minder and educator they actually liked.

They wouldn't need him.

Even sober, even without the added strain of a night of drinking and socializing in a decidedly uncivilized manner, he couldn't stomach more upheaval. Regardless of his motivations, which were selfish, he wanted his home to be a bastion of peace, *not a coop full of hens that squabble and peck at every given opportunity.*

Conversely, Reeve worried that Miss Sedgwyck might very well be one of those silly girls who presented more trouble than she was worth. He knew the type well: overeager to please, lacking two thoughts to fuse together in her head, and possibly looking to ensnare a duke into a liaison that might end in marriage.

Reeve had no objection to casual bedsport whatsoever, but for it to happen with a governess was shockingly unseemly. *Even to me.* Despite what the rumors stated about the *Duke of Havoc*, he would not indulge in such a thing.

So, it was with an uncomfortable mixture of hope and trepidation that Reeve and his daughters sat in the drawing room. One girl was on each side of him. All three of them were well groomed to wait upon the new addition to their household.

Once an agreement was reached, a date had been chosen for Miss Sedgwyck's arrival. Yesterday eve, Reeve had sent his carriage to collect her. The driver had arrived in York and was provided with accommodations for the night by the Sedgwycks. At dawn's first light, Reeve had instructed, the driver was to leave with Miss Caroline.

If his calculations were correct, and they always were, she should be arriving presently.

As if spurred by his thoughts, wheels clattered on the cobblestones outside. Their sound was muffled, as everything was for him, but even his sorry hearing could catch them. Reeve smiled to himself complacently.

Sophie, who caught the expression on her father's face, said with a frown, "What a peculiar smile, Papa. What's happened?"

Reeve could have ignored her and feigned that he had not heard her question. But knowing that the end to undertaking Lady Malliston's duties was near, he said, with good humor, "Nothing at all. I am just… thinking."

Thinking of his feminine savior, Miss Sedgwyck, who would relieve him of unnecessary monotony and the inconvenient shame he felt at being unable to genuinely connect with his children.

Why must I feel guilty about it?

He was tempted to rush to the window for a glimpse of their new arrival. However, he had instructed his daughters not to do so, and he did not relish the idea of their protests should he himself break the rule set for them.

They could be so persistent.

"Has she come, Papa?" Sophie asked.

"I believe we shall know soon enough."

Within the space of a few minutes, Mrs. Humphrey stalked into the room and her entire bearing radiated disapproval. Her gauntness only enhanced the look of utter distaste upon her face.

"Your *guest* has arrived, my lord."

At this announcement, but more than likely because she was terrified of the housekeeper, Phoebe sidled closer to Reeve and shoved her clammy little hand into his large one. He glanced at Sophie, whose eyes were fixed on the door behind Mrs. Humphrey.

Reeve refused to let Mrs. Humphrey's tone, which conveyed nothing but the greatest disdain, incense him. Since he had explained Miss Sedgwyck's hire and her purpose, Mrs. Humphrey and Miss Ball had, if it was possible, redoubled their efforts to treat him coldly. He didn't care one jot. In fact, he rather enjoyed rattling the old women.

Finally, he possessed enough leverage to make them squirm. The presence of new blood would demonstrate to them just how unneeded they really were.

He dangled the thought of their dismissal before them, and more insidiously, of their irrelevance to his household, with all the relish of a cat batting at a trapped mouse.

He would fondly remember the moment when they realized he was calling in Miss Sedgwyck, a replacement for Miss Ball. He'd summoned them both to his library, much as he had the day he'd returned home to find them up in arms against poor Duckie, and relayed in no uncertain terms that it was time to admit a new face would be more effective in the betterment of his daughters. Miss Ball could remain at The Thornlands, he'd said, but she would be sharing housekeeping duties with her sister.

At his words, Miss Ball had gone dangerously pale and he wondered with very little care if she might faint. He rather hoped she did.

Mrs. Humphrey's face resembled that of a gargoyle's, fierce and twisted.

"But," she'd protested, much more quietly than she should have – to rile him, of course, but he stepped closer to her with a wry expression, theatrically cupping his ear and leaning toward her – "We were practically family to Lady Malliston! You cannot simply see us out onto the streets just because your daughters refuse to abide by proper decorum."

Reeve didn't have to say he could. Both women knew full well that he was within his rights to dismiss them under whatever conditions he wished.

"Now, Mrs. Humphrey, when did I say I was throwing you out onto the streets? Cease your rambling, my dear woman, and count your blessings."

He was only bound by a strange, twisted sense of honor to his late lady wife, awful as she had been to him, to keep them in his service. He would, however, continue letting the thought of dismissal linger in their minds. They were old, dreadfully redundant, and only addled his home life in a way he did not appreciate.

In a perversely elegant manner, he thought, staring at Mrs. Humphrey, *it is similar to the way in which they held the threat of paddling over Sophie and Phoebe's heads.*

Miss Ball, who was apparently overwrought by the unexpected turn of events, had not emerged from her chamber all day. That was fine with Reeve, though he knew she was just sulking. He wanted everything to proceed without mishaps. The fewer people he had to concern himself with at the moment, the better.

"Even *I* could hear that, Mrs. Humphrey," he said, arching an eyebrow. "We shall wait here until she refreshes herself. She has traveled all day, after all."

"She has voiced no such wish to do so," said Mrs. Humphrey. She sounded as though she had just sipped pure lemon juice.

This gave Reeve some pause. Most young women Miss Sedgwyck's age would adhere to the reality, or the pretense, that they needed to retire to the room that had been prepared for them. They would probably maintain that they needed to attend to their toilette.

But not Arthur's daughter. Interesting.

Her looks were no concern of his, but it made Reeve surmise that she was older than he'd thought, which could indicate that she was not interested in the matter of her appearance.

Or perhaps she's just uncomely?

Either was just as well, but he hoped for his daughters' sake that she was, indeed, older, past girlish fripperies and vanities.

In the end, her education made more difference to him than her figure or her face. He did not think that Arthur had lied about her aptitude or her cleverness.

"Well. Thank you," he said to Mrs. Humphrey. He waved his marred hand in a clear but wordless dismissal, purposefully using his left to signify that he did not care what she thought of his imperfect physicality. "Have Edgar show her in."

Clearly, she understood he had no wish for her continued presence. The housekeeper quit the room with her narrow nose stuck in the air, and as she had been when she'd entered, she was still stalking. Reeve idly wondered if she'd ever walk like a woman of manners again, or if he had heaped too many indignities upon her by asserting his dominance over her and her sister.

On both sides, Sophie and Phoebe gave little, but audible, sighs of relief as she left. He squeezed Phoebe's hand. Surprised by the minute show of fatherly affection, she glanced sidelong at him. He was just as bemused that his hand seemed to have had a mind of its own, and immediately relinquished her hand when their eyes met.

Reeve fixed his attention to the doorway while straightening his back. *Why are you anxious? Don't be so absurd.*

There were easily a baker's dozen of ways this could go wrong; he wanted it to proceed perfectly. The battlefield never felt so complex to him as this banal matter of solving household problems. He could read offensive and defensive lines like words on a page.

By stark contrast, domestic matters stymied him.

Without consciously directing them, his eyes fell downwards.

When Edgar announced Miss Sedgwyck, Reeve was still contemplating the gleaming parquet panels.

Then she entered the room.

He glanced up only enough so that he would not appear either rude or nervous – truth be told, he could be both in social situations, now, so he readily employed rudeness to obscure the nerves – and inspected a pair of narrow feet in serviceable brown traveling boots.

He knew Arthur, like many old soldiers who did not have family money or titles, had fallen on hard times. These shoes attested to it. They were clean, but at least a few seasons old.

Above the boots was an equally practical fawn-colored dress to match. It was without much adornment, although there were newer cream lace accents that, perhaps, the owner had tatted and added herself to hide mending or new hems. Reeve eyed the dress before he took a proper look at Miss Sedgwyck. Like the boots, it was not new. He could not help but note that the dress, however plain it was, could not hide a fine, delicate figure. A simple white shawl was strewn over her shoulders and wrapped at her graceful neck, obscuring her bosom and shielding her from the slight chill in the air.

Perhaps she is not ugly.

At last, Reeve looked into her face. She looked nothing like her father, or what he recalled of the man; she must have favored her mother. Her dark eyes were striking, not that he could quite ascertain their color at this distance.

He hoped he did not look terribly taken aback. That would not do.

She was, in a word, beautiful, possessing the same fine features that he'd seen on ancient busts and statues during his travels. Even her frilly little cap, which was, like the rest of her garb, seasons out of date and an accessory that would have better suited his girls, not a woman grown, was not as unbecoming as it might have been on a less lovely creature. It contained most of her hair, but the rattling carriage, he imagined, had loosened some tendrils near her hairline.

As with her eyes, Reeve had some difficulty assessing its shade.

The fading light of day did not help him. It could be chestnut, or maybe auburn.

Not ugly, then.

For some reason, the way she had thwarted his lazy conjectures through no fault of her own other than possessing good attributes peeved him. He hoped the sigh he uttered was not too noticeable.

She did not need to retire to her room, or attend to herself in any way to become presentable for her new employer. Even after a long journey.

Reeve was a good judge of age. It came from practice, mostly, having had to estimate the age of younger men who had enlisted. Women presented only a slightly bigger challenge, if only because he had been exposed to fewer of them unless one counted ladies of ill repute. In their cases, life had rarely been kind to them and often made them look older than they were.

He guessed that Miss Sedgwyck was out of her teens, if only just. She had a calm bearing that befit an older woman, though.

Not that any of the women in The Thornlands were particularly dignified.

When Edgar, who lingered at the door, cleared his throat, Reeve knew he had stared for a little too long. He was thankful that his complexion, slightly browned from his time in military service and naturally inclined toward olive, would not give away his faint blush.

He quickly stood to receive her. Phoebe, unexpectedly, rose first, but Sophie readily followed her sister.

"My lord," Miss Sedgwyck said. She curtsied.

"Miss Sedgwyck."

Good Lord, was that a creak in his voice? And why on earth had her name come out as more of a question?

She could be no one else. He did not ever receive visitors.

At least I know my face is still inscrutable, thought Reeve. His show of surprise, however tiny, made him surly.

He had been told many times that his countenance was unreadable. It had been an endless point of contention between him and Lady Malliston, who would sigh and pout and insist he was being callous. He had quickly given up trying to explain to her that his face was just not a reliable way of reading his emotions.

In battle, it had always been an advantage.

It was an advantage, now.

"Yes, my lord," she said. If he was not mistaken, she sounded slightly confused. The half-question, half-statement present in the way he'd stated her name must have been more obvious than he'd hoped. "I am honored and pleased to be in your household at last."

Before he could reply, her eyes fell upon his daughters. "Are these to be my new pupils?"

Without waiting for his answer, she took a few paces forward, smiling at Phoebe and Sophie in turn.

"Yes," said Reeve. He indicated each girl with a hand upon her shoulder. "This is Sophie, my eldest, and Phoebe."

Bobbing shy curtsies that were less refined than he would have preferred – but he could only blame Miss Ball for that – the girls stepped toward Miss Sedgwyck.

She, to his surprise, went to her knees on the parquet floor so that she could be eye-to-eye with the little girls.

Even Edgar gave a sound of… was it approval? Disapproval?

Reeve couldn't be sure without seeing the man, and his ears certainly did not distinguish one emotion from the other without the help of his eyes.

"Aren't you girls just darling?" she said. "And as alike as two peas in a pod, too!" She beamed at them. "I am certain we shall have the most delightful time together."

Reeve had no idea how to reply to this show of what seemed to be genuine interest. He just stood there, a little behind the trio, and glanced over their heads at Edgar, who had the smallest of smiles on his old face.

On the other hand, Phoebe and Sophie seemed to know what to do.

"You are beautiful," Phoebe declared in her little voice.

Reeve only just caught it, and he only just caught it because he was rapt, trying to untangle what he was seeing and how he felt about it. He raised an eyebrow in surprise. Phoebe did not take to strangers. She took only to him, which he still didn't comprehend, and to Sophie.

"Thank you, Phoebe," said Miss Sedgwyck. She seemed truly pleased at the compliment, though it came only from a little girl.

"Will you paddle us... or shout at us?"

The question emerged from Sophie's lips in her usual blunt manner. It made Reeve's breath catch in his throat.

He coughed and, to his chagrin, discovered that he was rendered temporarily speechless.

He should be reining Sophie in, or apologizing to the new governess... anything to mitigate the barbarity implied in the innocent, but impertinent, query. He was already the *Duke of Havoc*.

He did not also need to be known as the "duke who had his daughters beaten at every infraction".

Miss Sedgwyck's beautiful face fell into an expression of disbelief, then pity. She said seriously to Sophie, who herself looked as serious as the grave, "You may have no doubt that I shall never hit or paddle you. Why anyone would ever want to do such a thing is beyond the pale."

She paused, seemingly to make sure Sophie and Phoebe were listening.

They were.

"My father and his sister, my Aunt Lydia, raised me. Never once have I been struck in punishment." Then, she smiled. "And believe me, I was not the easiest child in all of England."

Reeve was amazed when his girls gave each other a look... and giggled. Small giggles. But they were sounds of mirth and relief nonetheless.

"You would never cause mischief," said Phoebe with finality, as though her opinion settled the matter.

Reeve could have been knocked over by a feather. In actuality, he looked stiffer than a wooden plank, standing there rooted to the floor, the crook of his arm still raised against his mouth after his little coughing fit.

"I shall tell you later when we are better acquainted and you have no reason to think ill of me what sort of mischief I caused," said Miss Sedgwyck. "Though, you must promise never to let it give you ideas." She winked. Very minutely.

With that, Reeve knew his girls had accepted her.

Phoebe reached out her hand, which Miss Sedgwyck took readily, and Sophie, normally the more forward of the two, gazed up at her father before responding in kind. Reeve wondered if she could detect any of his thoughts. Probably not, although she generally had an uncanny ability to speak exactly the thing he wished to remain unsaid.

Then Sophie returned her attention to Miss Sedgwyck. She said, "I like you, Miss Sedgwyck."

"You may call me Miss Caroline, then."

Sophie nodded. "Miss Caroline."

Like she was an established financier about to strike a deal, Sophie offered her hand to Miss Sedgwyck, who relinquished Phoebe's to give it a firm shake. Even Reeve almost smiled at Sophie's gesture.

He had a sense that Miss Sedgwyck was his wisest decision yet, even if that decision only relieved him of having to tend to his daughters when he'd rather be seeking his fortune at the tables or his pleasure in a doxy's bed.

He found his voice at last. Reeve cleared his throat and said, "I am glad for your safe arrival, Miss Sedgwyck. I am equally pleased with the affection you seem to have kindled within my daughters. I daresay you shall find Sophie and Phoebe are most pleasant. Kindly do well by them."

His speech sounded stilted and a little too cold, even to his own blunted hearing.

Miss Sedgwyck relinquished her grasp on Sophie's hand and stood, brushing off the front of her fawn dress. "You have my word, Lord Malliston, that Sophie and Phoebe shall be treated as though they were my own flesh and blood. That means no paddling, either by my hand or some blunt object."

The mild jest was for the girls, but he might have sworn she directed it more at him.

So... she has spirit.

Satisfied, especially by her lack of affect, Reeve nodded. He did not quite smile but, still, he felt his face relax. In a brief, baffling moment, their eyes met and held – Reeve's brown against her dark green. Her eyes *were* green: he could see them better, now.

His usual strict composure slipped, as his instincts seemed to reaffirm without his better judgment's permission – *Yes, this is a very lovely young woman.*

She was first to look away, studying an old portrait of Reeve's father that had hung on the far wall for many years. He couldn't divine what she might be thinking. It didn't matter. It was not for him to know.

"Very well, then," he said. "Now that our first introductions have been made and you know Sophie and Phoebe..." he trailed off, and called more loudly than he intended, causing Edgar to jump out of a near stupor from his station by the door, "Duckie, do cease your lurking!"

The cook appeared immediately. She had been eavesdropping in the corridor. While Miss Sedgwyck had become acquainted with the girls, Reeve spied the toes of Duckie's worn shoes just past the doorjamb. It was still a mystery to him as to how such a rotund woman could sneak, then hide, but Duckie could.

He trusted her judge of character, and did not mind that she had taken it upon herself to listen to this first meeting.

Had it been either of his other female members of staff skulking about, his reaction would have been much different. But Duckie, unlike either Mrs. Humphrey or Miss Ball, cared deeply about Sophie and Phoebe. One might believe that because the sisters had been in Lady Malliston's service all of her life, they harbored warmth and affection toward her bereaved young children.

One would be entirely wrong.

While they were both positively reptilian in their inability to care and, indeed, in their ability to actively antagonize, Duckie seemed to want to make up for the girls' lack of a mother. She knew she couldn't, but she tried in her way all the same. If the grin creasing her broad face was any indication, she greatly approved of Miss Sedgwyck.

If Duckie approved, Reeve had no reason to disapprove.

"This is Mrs. Estelle Breem – Duckie – my cook," Reeve said, off Miss Sedgwyck's curious look. "She cares very much for Sophie and Phoebe."

Both women exchanged pleasantries and Duckie even gave a small curtsy. But before either could get carried away in the dictates of good manners or genuine conversation – *I think I've had enough conversing for one day* – he said, "Duckie, if you would show Miss Sedgwyck to her room and have a maid attend to her."

The duty should have been Mrs. Humphrey's. But Reeve preferred that the evening continue as affably as it had started. If Mrs. Humphrey was allowed to be alone in a room with Miss Sedgwyck, it was possible that he might be ordering someone to clean blood out of the carpets.

Whose, he could not say. Miss Sedgwyck did not seem the type to give up easily.

Sophie said, eagerly, "Shall *we* attend to her, too, Papa?"

Reeve was about to say no, that Miss Sedgwyck needed time to rest.

But the woman in question said, "That would be lovely, my lord. I wouldn't mind in the least, Sophie."

He was rather affronted that she had taken it upon herself to answer his daughter before he did. But then reflecting on the reasons for which he'd hired her, Reeve nodded.

"You may. But both of you must behave yourselves," he said.

He looked sternly down at Sophie, then at tiny Phoebe.

They beamed their pleasure at this pronouncement and it was settled. Duckie hurried the girls toward the door.

Miss Sedgwyck allowed them to precede her and lingered at the doorway before she quit the room. Edgar had followed Duckie, and the girls, who were issuing quiet squeals of delight. For the life of him, Reeve couldn't understand a syllable of what they said. He supposed it all had to do with the woman in front of him.

"I must thank you again, my lord, for this opportunity," she said, voice raised. "It will make all the difference to both my father and me." She paused, and then added hesitantly, but with clarity, "He does not speak much. He is a man of few words and is now a man of even fewer after the war. But when we received your letter, he spoke very highly of you. Understandably... I wanted to know his opinion of you."

Once again, Reeve found himself under her gaze. Rather, he looked down at her – a petite woman, she came only to his shoulder – and she up at him. There was almost a challenge in her eyes, but not quite. Because of that glint... a partial test, but more curiosity... he inferred that she, in a discreet way, referred to all the rumors that dogged him.

She said her father spoke well of him precisely *because* she knew many others did not.

In their very short acquaintance, he had detected strength of character and the quickness that her father had spoken of so proudly. Mischief lurked in her eyes, too. The lady herself had mentioned that her childhood was not always exemplary, and her gentle wit toward the girls hinted at an aspect of her nature he was not sure she'd ever really indulged.

He found himself wondering, quite abruptly, if she had been lonely in a house with only her aunt and father for companions. Impatiently, for it didn't truly matter to him, he brushed the thought aside.

She would be good for his daughters. That was all he needed from her.

"You are most welcome, Miss Sedgwyck," he said. "And thank you for relaying your father's sound regard. That is in rather short supply for me, as I'm sure you have come to know."

She merely quirked part of her mouth up in a half-smile and, after a low curtsy, she followed Duckie and the girls into the corridor where they waited.

Reeve was staring at the door for long moments after she left. Edgar summoned him back from his reverie.

"My lord?"

He had not entered the room, but instead waited on the other side of the doorway.

"Yes, Edgar?"

"Are you well?"

"Quite well, thank you," he said curtly.

"Very good, my lord," Edgar said. "The preparations for your upcoming gathering are in order."

The old butler's censure was mild, but still present. He said "gathering" with the tone reserved for words like "rubbish". It was Reeve's turn to host a party at The Thornlands for his friends and their array of bad habits.

Gambling, booze, women.

Even "party" might be too genteel a word, Reeve thought.

Luckily, The Thornlands was a large manor and could easily accommodate the raucous event without disturbing those who lived there and were not partaking. With Miss Sedgwyck finally present and soon to be settled, and the girls taking to her almost instantly, Reeve should have had an answer to some of his nightly prayers.

He should have been thanking his lucky stars, or God, or some combination of the two, and looking forward to the coming fun.

He should not have been thinking about a pair of glittering, clever, green eyes.

"Thank you, Edgar."

Edgar bowed and walked out of sight, leaving Reeve alone in the drawing room once more. Heaving a sigh, Reeve decided what he needed most was a strong drink, so he made his way to the library for a large brandy.

⁂

HER FIRST DINNER with Sophie and Phoebe was a pleasurable one. Caroline counted her blessings and tried not to seem too in awe of the glitter of fine china and cutlery, the warmth of candlelight on the dining room's intact, flowery wallpaper, or – most difficult of all – eat her courses too quickly.

She had not been raised poor, but recent times meant that even the simplest aspects of the duke's wealth, such as a well-laden table, threatened to overwhelm her.

Even her best evening dress was not quite up to standard, but neither Duckie nor the girls seemed to notice or comment. Instead of wondering what they might think of her faded lilac garment, Caroline gauged the girls' manners. They were completely satisfactory, if a little too rigid for such young children.

No doubt a result of the duke's own rather... cold... ways.

She tried not to judge him too sharply. War could do the strangest things to a man's mind, and so could the death of a beloved wife. Whatever the reason, she sensed he kept a distance between himself and his daughters, regardless of the pretty speech he had made in the drawing room earlier.

He had not joined them for dinner. This disappointed Caroline, who told herself she should not be so concerned over what her employer chose to do. It transpired that he was preparing himself for some grand party.

But the more Duckie nattered about it to Caroline, the less it sounded like a traditional party.

"Lord Malliston hosts his friends a few times during the year," the cook told her, as she personally filled Caroline's plate. For some reason, Duckie had taken to her as well as the girls had. "They'll arrive in the early hours of the morning, but you needn't worry about their presence in the manor. The number of rooms will suffice, and many provisions have been made to keep the men away from you and the girls, of course. They know not to wander about here." Duckie cocked her head, then, and added, "Perhaps your handsomeness might attract the men, anyhow. Best to keep to the family's wing, Miss Caroline. I wouldn't wander about. Meaning no disrespect."

"None taken, but…"

Duckie glanced at the girls, whose eyes were wide and ears were far sounder than their father's. It was apparent that she would say no more in front of them.

Caroline could make little sense of Duckie's blathering without more information. She supposed that the party would be largely male-dominated, which wasn't so surprising given the duke's widowed status.

To her mind, all Duckie meant was that there could be some men who, when they'd imbibed, might become too forward with an unattended young lady.

But that thought alone was absurd.

I shall be minding the girls, not mincing about a gathering full of strange men, thought Caroline.

She was not one to pry into others' affairs, perhaps because her own father was not exactly forthright about everything. As such, she allowed the matter to rest. The meal passed without any sight of the dour housekeeper – was that Miss Ball, or was it Mrs. Humphrey? *Mrs. Humphrey*, decided Caroline.

She was neither present to eat nor serve, so Caroline guessed she was occupied by preparations for the duke's coming guests. In truth, Caroline had little desire to see her again so soon. She was an odious woman, the type who had probably threatened Sophie and Phoebe with such violent punishment that they then had to ask a new adult charged with their care whether she would paddle them, too.

When they had all finished eating, Duckie shepherded the girls upstairs to their room, so Caroline had little choice but to do the same. She itched to explore her new home, but knew it would be beyond the bounds of propriety to do so. At the moment, she would not even have the excuse of, say, looking for the girls. Though prosaic, she had always had an exploratory streak.

She'd spent hours in her father's garden daydreaming about foreign lands and imaginary ones, so living in a grand, large house such as The Thornlands rekindled that old desire to explore.

She promptly ignored it.

It turned out that the room prepared for her was simple, but clean and elegant. It was near the girls' own, allowing her to hear them should they call out, and it was secluded well away from the servants' wing. She was encouraged that she wouldn't be near either the housekeeper, or the girls' old governess and tutor, whom she had not yet met.

While Duckie said that Miss Ball was indisposed, the turn of her lips said otherwise. Caroline knew without being told that Miss Ball was snubbing everyone.

A maid had helpfully left clean water and linen with which to wash her face and clean her teeth. After she'd tended to herself, put away her things, and settled on her bed, Caroline let her mind drift into introspection.

It had been such a strange, eventful day. She'd never been so far from her home and the entire journey here, she had been consumed with anxieties that had not made themselves real. She had not worried overmuch until she set off.

She was not given to dramatics or nervous shows of emotion, so she had kept everything to herself. But she had fretted that this was the wrong decision, that she should have remained with her father and found some other way to make ends meet. It was true that she would probably be bored. She was soundly educated, and there had been more than one time when her adept mind had been called unfeminine.

But if she'd stayed home, she wouldn't have had to navigate waters that, if she was being honest, frightened her. If her father had expressed any wish for her to remain with him before she'd gotten into the duke's carriage, she would have.

I wish I had the same faith in Lord Malliston that Father does, she thought, staring up at the ceiling. A lone candle provided her with enough light to barely see her surroundings.

She'd had to push all what-ifs to the side and concentrate on the good she was doing. They needed money, and so she went to The Thornlands. But the further she came to be from her childhood home, the easier it was for doubt to seep into her mind. What if she was blundering into the home of a murderer?

Unlike Father, she thought, *I cannot dismiss the idea so readily.*

Having now met the man, she could almost leave the thought behind. But there was something distant and alien in his eyes, and it prompted her back to wondering – what was the truth, if there was any, to the rumors? He held himself like nobility, like a member of the *ton*, but there was something distinctly amiss about him, too.

It was possible, she conceded, that his lack of hearing had created this difference. He had not grown up with the impairment.

It must be bizarre, Caroline thought, *and tragic to have that taken from you.*

But then, it was significant that he could not obtain a new tutor from within Easingwold. That meant his reputation was very marked among the locals, marked enough to necessitate him to ask her father, who was not well connected within society and scarcely affiliated with a member of the nobility, if he could employ *her.*

To a lesser extent, she was worried about the girls and how they might behave in her care. She hadn't lied when she told them she wasn't the easiest child. She knew what tricks little girls – and older ones – could get up to, and her father's patience paired with her aunt's influence had been the perfect combination to ensure she grew up properly.

And thank God that Mama expressed her wish that her children be educated.

Many times, her father had told her that as soon as Lily discovered she was with child, they discussed how that child, regardless of sex, should be well read and well taught in things like mathematics, botany, French, and even politics and law, so far as those things could be managed. True to Lily's wish, Caroline received a thorough grounding in many subjects.

Despite knowing she was more than capable of a tutor's duties, Caroline's worries only heightened upon her arrival at the manor.

The Thornlands was a grand estate, and the enormous grounds intimidated her as soon as she had been transported through them. She was the daughter of a teacher who laid no claim to wealth, but she had been privileged enough to occasionally accompany him to the ornate, expansive homes of his pupils. During these visits, which weren't numerous, she'd discovered that the gentry were not generally keen on rubbing shoulders with those they deemed beneath them.

Some were just more polite about it than others.

This was made painfully clear by her several shouting matches with young ladies, her father's pupils, who declared that she had no right to be in their houses, even if her father was *providing a service.*

One such argument ended with Caroline backing a girl into a corner and giving her a black eye. Fortuitously, the girl's father, who'd been with Arthur in the drawing room while the spat developed in the second parlor, had overheard everything.

He magnanimously declared that his dear Rosie—*Lady* Rosie—had unfairly baited Caroline.

Thus, Caroline's father did not lose any business.

Caroline, however, lost the treat of being able to go with Arthur.

She chuckled to herself, thinking over that particular lesson.

Deep down, Caroline was concerned that, perhaps, Lord Malliston might arrive at the conclusion that she was an upstart, an opportunist.

She normally felt no shame about her own station. She considered herself fortunate, and her only oddity was the book learning upon which her late mother had insisted. It was strange for a girl child, especially a girl child who was not of noble birth, to be so learned.

But her father had found tutors and bartered his skills for theirs, and Caroline was somewhat of an autodidact who enjoyed teaching herself things. Books had helped her learn where people could not.

Despite her myriad of fears, she was able to approach the house with a calm, if tense, dignity.

She was then received by the butler, an agreeable old man called Edgar, and the housekeeper, Mrs. Humphrey, a disagreeable old woman if ever she had seen one.

However, all thoughts and lingering perceptions of both Edgar and Mrs. Humphrey vanished as soon as she stepped into Lord Malliston's drawing room.

And it wasn't because it was a fine room.

While Caroline had met men who were pleasing to the eye, she hadn't met one who'd caught hers as much as the Duke of Nidderdale.

It was inconvenient.

She was very surprised by her reaction. Her father had relayed that he was about thirty, or somewhat past it, and of good health with the exception of his hearing and his left hand, of course, which had both suffered in battle.

So, she did not necessarily expect an "ugly" man, but neither did she expect one who was so attractive. She had not thought her mouth would go dry at the sight of him.

Just nerves, she'd thought. That was an outright lie she was still telling herself, hours later, to drive the duke from her mind's eye.

Though he had been sitting with his daughters when she first entered, she judged by the span of his shoulders that he was not a small man. Her guess was proven correct when he stood. Lord Malliston was tall, taller than many men in Caroline's acquaintance.

At the time, she wondered if the pleasant hue of his skin was due to time spent in the sun or a natural inclination. She suspected that, given these months of being indoors, it was the latter. Perhaps he had something other than English ancestry in his blood. He boasted a handsome face with high cheekbones, and his physique was lean but not what she would call thin. His daughters, on the other hand, must have taken more after their mother.

She wondered, in that moment, why he hadn't married again. Perhaps he *had* murdered his wife. Otherwise, how else could he have remained unmarried? There were few women's heads he would not turn, she was certain of it. Her closest friend, Viola, who had a history of becoming infatuated with every handsome man she met, would be mute in his presence.

Then, seeing the duke's daughters drove her rather shocking thoughts from her head.

Their expressions spoke of fretful expectation and the trepidation in their eyes wrenched at her heart.

Caroline nearly, but did not quite, forget about the duke in her bid to reassure them, and their warmth toward her allayed some of her own fears. Soon enough, she was thankful that these two girls were her new charges and thinking again that her employment could signify good fortune. She hadn't expected to gain their affection so quickly, if at all.

Maybe it's meant to be.

The girls barely allowed her the time to have a bath and change clothing before they took her on a spirited tour of The Thornlands.

They started with the inner rooms, where the wealth of her new employer was rendered even more obvious. It wasn't that the duke's tastes were garish. Far from it. It was, quite simply, that everything, from the paintings to the vases to the furniture, was of the highest standard, and each item was beautifully crafted.

Then, they reached the dining room.

On the far wall, Caroline observed a portrait of a pale, golden-haired lady with blue eyes. Something about the unknown woman unsettled her. On closer inspection, she must have been Phoebe and Sophie's mother because the resemblance was so strong.

Tentatively, Caroline asked if this was the case, reluctant to upset either girl, but too curious not to inquire.

Sophie blandly informed her that, yes, it was. Interestingly, it seemed that neither she nor her sister were overly saddened by their mother's death. Caroline could not say if that was because they had been even younger than they were now when she passed, and thus could not exactly remember their mother. She knew that, for her own part, even though she could not even remember her mother, thinking about Lily left her with a warm glow.

Caroline stopped staring at the portrait and quickly asked to be shown the grounds. She needn't have worried about her possible *faux pas* because neither girl realized how uncomfortable she was.

Phoebe grabbed her skirt and led the way for them to go outside.

Even outdoors, she couldn't help but imagine the late Lady Malliston's striking blue eyes were watching her, boring through the walls and glass to peer upon her…

Ultimately, Caroline decided to try not to think about the portrait again and, all through dinner, she resolved not to look at it, either.

Father must be right. He's almost always right, she thought, as the shadows flickered on her ceiling. The problem was, she was often right, too, and only one of them could be correct about Lady Malliston's fate. She didn't want to think that the man who'd so distracted her had murdered his own wife.

She sighed.

First thing in the morning, she would write to her father. He would want to know how she had fared on her journey. It was premature, yet, to tell him how she felt about living at The Thornlands. But she could let him know she was well, and that the young girls were lovely. After she sent the letter, she would take to her duties.

Evidently, the duke was friendly enough to host friends and neighbors in his house. Could he really be as bad as people said?

Lord Malliston is bound to be the good man Papa deemed him to be. How could he have raised Sophie and Phoebe, otherwise? she thought sternly, trying to take control of her mind.

Over time, she would come to a better understanding of the situation. She was confident, too, that she'd become a valued member of the household.

Chapter Five

I N THE SPACE of two days, Caroline stopped trying to think well of the Duke of Nidderdale.

He was, perhaps, the worst father she'd ever encountered.

Fuming, trying to keep a handle on her emotions, she passed through the garden in search of Lord Malliston. In far less than half a week, he'd proven himself a selfish, thoughtless man who gave very little care to his girls.

It's only been two days, she thought with amazement. *Barely two days.*

Oh, he *had* performed well on the afternoon she arrived, providing the illusion that he was simply an aloof man with more affairs than just his children to attend to. And despite his lack of contact with his daughters, he appeared to mind very much who looked after them.

Nothing could be further from the truth.

Sophie and Phoebe had only continued to endear themselves to Caroline, but their father had inspired a fury that displaced her initial intrigue. She was so furious that she no longer wondered who had killed Lady Malliston, not because she believed he had, but because his other foibles were sharply obvious.

It wasn't her place and she shouldn't have been possessed by the desire to shake him at the shoulders until his teeth rattled.

Not that I could even if we were friends, she thought, twitching up her skirts as she walked through a thick carpet of dead leaves.

Lord Malliston was much larger than her. She would need to stand on a chair to even reach his shoulders, much less to shake him.

When Duckie had told her of his upcoming party, she thought the duke was only trying to rekindle goodwill between him and the local gentry. At the time, she'd thought it noble of him to try.

How naïve of me.

Duckie's words had been laced with enough hints. She was merely too inexperienced to comprehend them. She was not a simple woman. But due to her father's place in life and their lack of both wealth and connections, she had not been exposed to very much of the world. There hadn't been the opportunities for her to experience the ways of men or understand their tastes.

With dismay, Caroline had come to realize that the duke's friends, none of whom seemed to be directly local, were raucous and lewd.

She, still trying to believe the best about Lord Malliston, had originally thought Duckie's warning to not be seen by "the men" was too zealous. Therefore, she hadn't chosen to be more covert. Apart from that, The Thornlands was so large and complex she was still learning the multiple ways to move about the manor and grounds. It was not easy to remember the more private ways to and fro.

After settling the children in their beds, Caroline had taken a leisurely, chilly walk in the garden. Feeling refreshed, she then wanted to retire for the night. On her way inside, she encountered a man just entering the manor, struggling with his bags, and surmised that he was a late arrival to the duke's party. Lord Malliston did not employ a large number of staff, so no one was present to relieve this stranger of his baggage or direct him.

Raised by both Aunt Lydia and her father to be polite, she greeted him deferentially. It would have been rude not to, for she was directly in his sight. She was rewarded for her efforts with a lascivious wink and a quietly uttered, but clearly meant, remark. Astonished by his crude behavior, Caroline hurried to her room without making anything of it. He might have been intoxicated already. Although that was not an excuse, inebriation could lead even the best men down a path that they might regret.

While she could have permitted the one slight toward her, Caroline refused to overlook the presence of dubiously reputed ladies in the manor. She had woken and discovered not just one, but at least three, strange women garbed in risqué attire floating about The Thornlands. None of them slighted her. They greeted her with courtesy, and she tried to be courteous in return. One was quite sweet, asking Caroline where she might find Duckie, whom she appeared to remember fondly from another one of these gatherings.

What Lord Malliston chose to do in privacy and seclusion was his own business. This, though, was beyond her comprehension. Caroline could not believe the duke solicited the custom of strange women while his own family was home.

What if Sophie or Phoebe came across one of these ladies? Of course, she made sure that the girls did not wander at will, but they could easily toddle from their rooms to the rest of the house without an adult noticing for quite some time. It was such a vast estate.

It wasn't exactly the ladies who bothered Caroline. She supposed that everyone had to make their way in the world, somehow.

It was what the girls might see them doing with the men that concerned her. Not only were they far too young to encounter such adult things, there was also a proper context in which they should learn about them.

Later, too, she thought.

How was she to know that the duke's party was a gambling and – she cringed as she thought the word – *whoring* party?

Caroline was so embroiled by her annoyance that it was too late when she caught the sounds.

Slowly, she noticed that the closer she came to the heart of the garden, the more distinctly she heard soft gasps and little, breathless laughs. They came from both a man and a woman. This was not surprising given the purpose of Lord Malliston's party – and they were clearly *engaged*. The foliage was still too plentiful for her to see anything.

Caroline was relieved, but slightly disappointed, that it shielded her.

She found it unlikely that the man in question was the duke. Surely even he, with all his apparent proclivities for the improper, would not engage in relations in his own garden. This must be one of his wonderful friends.

It is broad daylight, and winter, for heaven's sake!

Although she was blushing, she found the whole situation ridiculous. This was modern England and there shouldn't be any room for bacchanals in gardens.

She kept treading forward, seething, avoiding the living plants at her toes as well as she could. It was an unseasonably mild winter that felt more like autumn, which she supposed had partially encouraged this liaison's outdoor venue.

She didn't see the duo until she was well within the secluded garden's center. Caroline was ready to give them quite a dressing down, whether or not it was strictly her own purview to do so.

What if one of the maids or Duckie had decided to take the girls out for a morning constitutional? Fornicating in a bedchamber was one thing, but this was another matter!

Caroline kept marching right up to the amorous pair.

Then she realized who the man was, and stopped dead, caught between horror and... *Caroline Sedgwyck, you cannot possibly be jealous of a common doxy.*

The nagging taint of jealousy brought with it shame, and inexplicably, anger.

Lord Malliston sat on the very bench she'd occupied last evening, gazing up at the clear twilight skies and thanking her good fortune. But upon his lap there was a raven-haired woman with her skirts drawn up to her thighs, and it was very obvious that they were – there was no other way that Caroline, so flustered, could put it – enjoying each other's company. Intimately. The duke's face rested against the woman's exposed bosom, which he was nuzzling, eliciting the lady's groans of pleasure. When he shifted his right hand under her skirts, moving it deftly, Caroline gawped with morbid curiosity.

Whatever he was doing, his companion was appreciative.

Even though Caroline had never happened upon such a sight in all her years, she was not ignorant of what she was witnessing. Neither her father nor her aunt knew, but once she had entered her teens, she started to indulge in books they would have surely deemed inappropriate. She had simply secreted them out of sight and read them under the cover of darkness after everyone had gone to bed, with only a low candle for weak light.

What she had not done, however, was engage in any activities the books described.

Although she wanted to attribute the warmth in her cheeks to pure mortification, she couldn't. While she was startled by the sight and angry at its ramifications for the duke's girls, her disloyal body seemed to be responding in a way that was not unfavorable.

After a few moments, she gave a rather loud, affronted noise of confusion, and it was even enough for the duke to glance up, startled, looking over the woman's pale shoulder.

His brown eyes met Caroline's.

Then he flew to his feet, causing his lover to tumble off his lap, and the bench, in a tangle of cerulean skirts. She hit the ground with a grunt of pain, but neither Lord Malliston nor Caroline acknowledged it.

Caroline could not stop looking at him, even as he struggled with his trousers. Her eyes ranged no lower than his face, and she made no attempt to disguise the mingled disappointment and uncertainty that had to be legible in her expression.

She prayed that if she exhibited anything less than fitting for a respectable woman, whether that was pique or – Heaven forbid – lust, it was not evident to him.

"Do you know no shame?" she said finally. Caroline gestured behind herself toward the manor. "Your own daughters are in there!"

He did not respond; he just stared at her.

She sighed and ignored the woman who was still sitting on the ground and fixing her dress so that she was not exposed. "You could have at least sought out this kind of company elsewhere! If you must have it. Perhaps all the rumors about you *are* true, my lord."

Careful, Caroline, she thought. *You're neither his wife nor his family. You are not even his friend.*

She decided it would be better to turn heel and go back the way she came. With as much dignity as she could muster, she shook her head and started off. Her mind was whirling.

Could she stay under his roof if he was so irresponsible? What might happen to Sophie or Phoebe if she left?

Duckie had made it seem like these parties were infrequent, which was only a small blessing. Caroline knew there had been more than one.

She hadn't gone three feet before the duke caught up with her.

She kept walking, but his legs were long and he kept pace with her easily.

"Miss Sedgwyck," he said.

She kept silent, her lips pursed.

"Miss Sedgwyck," he repeated.

Now, he was walking by her side, the woman with whom he had just been intimate apparently all but forgotten. This raised her ire, again, and she came to a halt, fixing him with what she intended to be a cold look. *Is that how he regards us women?* she thought.

"I have nothing to say to you, my lord," she said.

The nicety tasted sour on her tongue.

"But I have something to say to you," Lord Malliston said. He was calm, but there was a tight set to his well-defined, thin lips that belied his nerves.

Caroline crossed her arms, hugging herself. "You may say it, if you wish. But do not take too long. I wouldn't want to keep you from your paramour."

She couldn't resist making the jibe.

Lord Malliston sighed. He said, "First, I am... extremely sorry that you happened upon me and ah, my... friend. Believe me, had I known someone would venture close, we would have found a more... discreet place."

Caroline blanched. "That's all you are sorry for? That someone came across you? My lord, the issue was not that you weren't in a *discreet place.*"

He scowled. "That is not your assessment to make."

She would have none of it. He taxed her self-control.

"Save your apologies, Lord Malliston," she said. The honorific, though still acrid in her mouth, helped her sound as deferential as she should have been. "I am in no way connected to your family. Of course I have no right to judge you. You may do whatever you desire in any corner of The Thornlands. But if I was *a father*, I would reconsider my behavior when it might badly impact my children." Agitated, she started to pace in front of him. "On top of your coldness toward Sophie and Phoebe which, by the way, *I* even noticed – me, a stranger – with these *parties*, you place them in circumstances that may lead them to abuse or moral confusion. You have a responsibility, my lord, to ensure they are safe and well-educated in how to comport themselves as titled young ladies."

He stared at her, affronted, but she was not done.

"That's neither here nor there, though... I cannot be a governess or a tutor in the midst of such..." she searched for words. "Debauchery. Negligence. I shall ask Edgar that my trunk be packed within the hour. If you will be so kind as to permit your driver to take me back to –"

Lord Malliston interrupted her sharply. "You are declaring that you will abandon your post?"

"*That* is what rouses a response from you?" But if Caroline was not mistaken, there was new contrition sneaking onto his angular, elegant face. "*Yes.*"

"Whatever for? I thought you liked the girls as much as they adore you. Was I wrong in this supposition?"

There was enough puzzlement in the duke's glinting, amber-brown eyes to cause Caroline to have yet more visions of shaking him until his teeth rattled, the lack of a convenient chair for her to stand upon be damned.

How could he not understand her chagrin?

Instead of inflicting violence against his person, she settled for breathing an exasperated sigh.

"You must understand that I have no complaints about the girls. They are nearly perfect charges," she said.

Perhaps instead of shaking him, I could kick him in the shins.

"Then you wish to go on my account."

"Finally, you are speaking with some sense." It was bold of her, but she could not curtail her tongue.

The duke's abandoned paramour emerged at that moment.

Fuming angrily and tossing a vitriolic glare in Caroline's direction, she toddled in the general direction of the manor. She conspicuously lacked stockings, and Caroline knew that a woman of her profession would not bother to wear any out of the house in the first place. But she may as well have been nonexistent for all the attention Lord Malliston accorded her very pointed departure.

"You must not go, Miss Sedgwyck," he said. "If you do, you will have broken an agreement between three parties – you, me, and your father – and you will no doubt cause a heartbreak for my poor daughters. They decidedly latched on to you from the very first day."

He is shrewd, Caroline thought. *Using the girls as leverage.*

"You may well be assured, my lord, that my father and I shall refund the advance payment you have made to him," Caroline said calmly. In truth, she did not know if that was possible. In all likelihood, her father had already spent a little of the money. It had been so sorely needed.

"But my daughters – you will abandon them? Are you that indifferent to their innocent feelings, Miss Sedgwyck?"

"What, as you are, my lord?" she said with incredulity. His unashamed use of his daughters as bargaining chips infuriated Caroline, and anger loosened her speech again. She flung out her arms for emphasis.

"Upon my honor, you are the most hypocritical man I have ever had the misfortune to meet. Don't you dare accuse me of the same detachment and disinterest you yourself exhibit! You have visited your girls only once since I arrived here – to instruct them to keep away from the drawing room and the parlors and the dining room so your *friends* would not be embarrassed by their presence. Several days have passed since I came to The Thornlands, and the *concerned father* could not bring himself to ask the new tutor how his daughters were faring." She laughed derisively.

He was gaping at her, but she was not finished.

She could not quite meet his eyes, but she was determined that he would understand her thoughts.

"You hold a gambling party with the little ones under your roof! While you may suppose that they have no idea what you and your lot are about, you must abandon that notion. Phoebe asked me this morning at breakfast why *those* ladies did not dress like I do." She eyed the woman who was still walking toward the manor. "As I sat there, unable to think of anything sensible to say, Sophie declared that she *preferred* the other ladies' attire. She was particularly entranced by the rouge on their faces, too. Just imagine if one of your daughters had caught you in my place. My lord, what on earth would you have told her by way of explanation?"

At the end of her long speech, Caroline was not displeased to find that her audience of one was staring at her in astonishment. She was also, she realized, only a pace or two away from him.

Surely, now, I will be asked to leave the manor, Caroline thought.

Her anger was short-lived as it always was, but it always presented itself forcefully when she had lost her temper. She had invoked enough fury to upset any man, much less an employer who was of the gentry.

She had spoken nothing but the truth, but perhaps it was not her place to do so. She was only a tutor. Teachers, she should have learned from her father's experience, never remarked upon what transpired in their employers' lives.

Heavens, this is as bad as hitting Lady Rosie in the parlor when I was fifteen, she thought.

She began to worry in earnest when the duke remained silent for what felt like hours.

"Forgive me," she said, only to break the silence. She did not actually think she needed to be forgiven. "My words were harsh, although I believe they were the truth."

"You owe me no apologies for telling the truth," the duke said quietly. He had taken a small step toward her, and now there was only one pace between them.

His mild words shocked Caroline. She waited as he composed himself.

"It must appear to you that I am irredeemable. But I promise that I have only ever wanted the best for my daughters." He paused. "I would not have engaged your services otherwise. In the past, I have thought that Sophie and Phoebe were well hidden from my parties by the women of the house. By Duckie and Miss Ball and Mrs. Humphrey, I mean to say."

"Perhaps," Caroline said tiredly, "you misjudge their intelligence and natural curiosity, my lord. They are no longer babes in the cradle."

He nodded. "No. They have grown more than I can fathom... even in these months since..."

Since their mother died, Caroline mentally finished for him.

Lord Malliston resumed speaking after a moment of quiet. "Sophie, in particular, must not be encouraged along in those... thoughts of hers. Thank you for telling me of my daughters' interest in my affairs, Miss Sedgwyck. I would not have known otherwise. I shall rectify the affair immediately."

It occurred to Caroline that despite the duke being prone to debauched behavior, he was actually quite awkward and even gruff. The traits did not seem to coincide.

Caroline blinked at his back as he began to walk away, trying not to linger on the intriguing lines of his shoulders under his coat.

She did not understand what the duke now intended to do. "My lord?" she called hesitantly.

"I presume that if the objectionable activities are taken away from here, you shall not actually be leaving my employ," he said, quite abruptly, whirling back to her.

Caroline wanted to say something in response. She did not know what that should be or even what further censure she could offer without being rebuked herself.

The duke interpreted her silence as an assent.

Smirking at her, he continued on his way into the house, leaving Caroline sufficiently flummoxed.

"IT IS NOTHING short of delightful to know that you are not only handsome, you also have a good head on your shoulders – more young ladies your age ought to have 'em."

It was time for luncheon, and ever since the party left the manor the day prior, Duckie had been filled with nothing but effusive praise for the new tutor. She perceived that Caroline, being the only new factor within The Thornlands, could be the only reason for this agreeable turn of events. In her honor, Duckie prepared a veritable feast for lunch.

Caroline could already tell this brought disdain from the other women of the house. Mrs. Humphrey and Miss Ball were seated at the table with them.

Duckie herself would never sit at the table with any of them. In her own firm words, she explained, "I have my place in the kitchen. I see no point in sitting down formal-like just to put food in my stomach."

Nonetheless, she took it upon herself to wait upon the diners, hovering to cater to their needs. This attentive service was entirely for Caroline's sake, as well as Phoebe and Sophie's. Even in her short residency at The Thornlands, Caroline knew the cook and the sisters never saw eye to eye.

Uncomfortable, Caroline said, "Duckie, you must not praise me. I have only done my duty to the girls in pointing out the impropriety of having such a party here." She reddened slightly.

She had, in fact, been thinking back to Lord Malliston's exposed thighs in the garden rather too much to claim any credit for her supposed moral righteousness.

"And not many people would deign to do that," said Duckie stoutly. "None, I would wager."

With the exception for Duckie's warm words toward Caroline, they were all awkwardly seated at the table in a silence laden with disgruntlement. Miss Ball sat beside Mrs. Humphrey, and both sisters looked like they would take immense delight in castigating Duckie for anything they could deem subpar. They glared at their food, at Sophie and Phoebe, and especially at Caroline.

She had decided not to take notice of this, but would have greatly preferred it if Duckie would keep her kind words to herself. They were sweet and Duckie meant well, but it all only increased the divide between the sisters, Duckie, and Caroline, who had only just become part of daily life at The Thornlands.

In the few days that Caroline had been present at the manor, Miss Ball and Mrs. Humphrey had not ingratiated themselves to her in the least. Quite the contrary, through their words – or lack thereof, depending on their moods – and by their actions, they revealed to her just how offended they remained at her mere presence in the house. Only Duckie's affable reassurance heartened Caroline a little. Duckie bolstered her fortitude by ignoring the women's ill tempers. This, Caroline felt, was a particularly brilliant solution.

Women like them only want attention, she thought.

"Sophie, Phoebe... shall we take our lessons in the garden, this afternoon?" she asked, hoping to break the tense atmosphere. "The fresh air can only help us."

"Can we?" said Sophie rapturously. "I love to sit in the gardens, Miss Caroline!"

"We were never allowed to play in the garden," said Phoebe, though the joy wrought by Caroline's suggestion was evident in her eager expression.

However, Miss Ball appeared quite flabbergasted at the idea.

"Children should not be given such liberty with their lessons," she declared. She shoveled a piece of chicken into her thin mouth, then took her time to chew and swallow before saying, "Phoebe already supposes they are going to the gardens to *play*. How will any substantial lessons be taught in such a distracting place, Miss Sedgwyck?"

"My dearest Anna, I daresay that it is nothing but inexperience and vapidity that leads young Miss Sedgwyck to such a suggestion." Mrs. Humphrey spoke before Caroline could answer. "Personally, I will continue to insist that the job of coaching young girls should be left to the sensible and experienced. But alas, the duke seems to confuse pretentious superciliousness with true intelligence."

Caroline was too stunned to make a reply. Quietly, she stared at Lady Malliston's portrait, which was directly across from her on the wall. The pale eyes of the late Lady stared back at her accusingly – as if to tell her that she deserved every abuse hurled in her direction.

Only Duckie gasped at the remarks, her hands fluttering about in high indignation.

"How rude you are, Mrs. Humphrey!" she exclaimed in an offended voice. "You must apologize to Miss Caroline this instant." Amongst the three female staff of the household, only Duckie called Caroline "Miss Caroline".

"Of course, I will do no such thing," Mrs. Humphrey replied, utterly unbothered. "I will make no apologies for my open nature and genuine frankness of character, which, if I might add – and I daresay that I can – is in contrast to the brazen disrespect that I suffer in this house. Some people, I declare, possess such ill-breeding as to repulse me."

Her eyes glittered maliciously at Caroline.

The look of such gobsmacked affront on Duckie's face was almost all it took for Caroline to regain her composure.

Perhaps, it was Miss Ball's barely concealed giggle following her sister's hurtful words. Or perhaps, it was the mirrored expressions of extreme discomfort on Sophie and Phoebe's young faces – faces that, only a few minutes ago, had been filled with interest and glee. Caroline quickly decided that ignoring Mrs. Humphrey and Miss Ball would not stop their endless provocations.

Should she continue to remain silent, they would perceive her as a target. Already, they believed her as pretentious.

With a smile on her face, a smile that she wore only for Sophie and Phoebe's sakes, Caroline looked in the direction of Mrs. Humphrey and her sister. "You see, *Madame*, as much as I would have been inclined to respect an opinion offered by such a sensible and experienced lady as yourself, I would much rather not. It is *my* opinion that good breeding can be found in many places, and amongst many people. Regardless of their stations. However, it would *never* lead one to continue to rain insults upon a new member of the household, and further... it would prevent such nasty bile being dripped in front of children."

Caroline's words were uttered with such a benign smile that she got no response from those to whom it was directed. Even Duckie, who always had something to say even if it was nonsense, found herself silent.

The stunned silence continued until the end of the meal, when Caroline serenely ushered her wards out of the room.

When she was at the door, she barely heard Miss Ball say to Mrs. Humphrey in a tiny voice, "Why, were you just abused by that miss, Isabelle?"

Caroline firmly shut the door on her way out.

"MRS. HUMPHREY IS going to take a paddle to you."

The children and Caroline had just settled in the garden and were set to begin their lessons when Phoebe made this solemn announcement. Startled by the suddenness of this, and thinking it to be Phoebe's attempt at joking, Caroline burst into amused laughter.

Her giggles died a quick death when she caught the solemn look on both her wards' little faces.

"Of course she would not!" she said. "Why would you even think so?"

"When Mrs. Humphrey gets angry, she threatens to paddle our backsides. I imagine she might want to do the same to you," Sophie said, wide-eyed.

"And she seems pretty angry, too," added Phoebe.

Caroline saw that the girls were truly concerned for her. They were filled with the sincere fear that she would, indeed, get herself beaten by the irksome housekeeper.

"Has Mrs. Humphrey ever taken a paddle to your backsides?" she asked the girls, looking closely at them.

Her question solicited a telling silence from both of them. Sophie suddenly developed an avid interest in studying her fingers, while Phoebe stuck her thumb in her mouth, and began to suck as though she hadn't eaten any noon meal at all.

"Phoebe... Sophie?" Caroline said. "If Mrs. Humphrey ever did, you would tell me, wouldn't you?"

She received no answer from either girl.

Fearing the worst, Caroline decided to lay the matter to rest for now. While she had decided on civility and firmness with the two sisters, this new knowledge, unconfirmed though it was, was sufficient bait to abandon the more rational decision immediately. In fact, Caroline wanted to march back into the house and take a paddle to Mrs. Humphrey's backside herself. She could not imagine why anybody would ever raise a hand against the girls.

It would seem that she would have to have yet another frank talk with the reprobate duke whenever he returned from his gambling party.

She only hoped she would not catch him in *flagrante delicto*, first, next time.

Chapter Six

M ISS ANNA BALL and Mrs. Humphrey came to be known as the Witch Sisters.

Duckie coined the sobriquet in one of her more sprightly moods. While Caroline was not inclined toward nursing uncharitable thoughts about others, she accepted that it was apt. She just endeavored never to use it around the children. Now that she suspected that one or both of the sisters had physically disciplined Phoebe and Sophie, she could not actively try to think of them with any kindness.

Caroline's response to the sisters' rudeness had finally been understood as the insult that it truly was meant to be, and the Witch Sisters, having decided that Caroline did not hold them in any esteem at all, rallied to regain their authority in the house. By and by, they resolved to ensure that the *little snobbish miss* was put in her place.

One evening, when Caroline was passing through the kitchen to pour herself a glass of water – she was not a servant, but did not think herself above those tasks – she overheard a conversation between the sisters that made their position toward her perfectly clear. It was as though they assumed everyone in the house, not just Lord Malliston, was hard of hearing and spoke too freely.

But Caroline, with keen ears that had not suffered in battle, heard everything, pausing in a nook between the kitchen and the ground floor solar that the sisters so liked to use as their own.

"Why, she is *a nobody* with designs on the duke himself!" said Mrs.

Humphrey.

"That's the only reason she seeks to endear herself to his daughters," said Miss Ball, "and dispose of his poor, dead lady wife's most loyal friends!"

"That," said Mrs. Humphrey, "will happen over *my* dead body, Sister."

Caroline could neither forget nor forgive what she had heard. But she did not announce her presence, instead making her way back upstairs as silent as a mouse.

And now, for what seemed like the thousandth time in a fortnight, Caroline found herself at loggerheads with the Witch Sisters.

After dinner, Caroline had ventured near the grand pianoforte that sat in a corner of the drawing room, admiring its beauty. She ran a gentle finger along the keyboard, closing her eyes at the perfectly tuned, lovely notes it produced. She was not even actually playing.

Caroline's eyes opened to meet Miss Ball's dark glare.

She had been quietly enjoying a game of whist with her sister, but the idea of Caroline even briefly touching the pianoforte seemed to induce a nearly apoplectic rage. Miss Ball's horsey face was beet red.

"Miss Sedgwyck, you must desist! That is not to be played by anyone in the house."

"Why ever not? It is such a grand instrument."

Mrs. Humphrey took the responsibility of addressing Caroline's evidently woeful ignorance on the matter.

"The pianoforte is the duke's favorite instrument in the house," she said, as though she was speaking to an errant child. "He loved to play and did so extraordinarily well – much to the delight of us all. Particularly our dear lady. But he went off to war and lost two of his fingers right along with much of his hearing. He would not go near the instrument again." Her eyes flashed in warning. "We *never* play in deference to this loss, so you must ensure never to do so, too."

Indeed, Caroline knew that the duke's left hand was missing its two middle fingers. She had observed it. Her father had also mentioned this to her.

"The duke always has my sympathies, for he has endured much that we ladies will never know. But surely he would enjoy hearing music in his manor again instead of letting such a gorgeous instrument go to waste. It isn't meant to be a decoration."

"That would be most uncaring of you," said Miss Ball. She wrinkled her nose like she suddenly smelled excrement. "Most uncaring, indeed."

"To think that one would so callously play when he cannot!" said Mrs. Humphrey. "You are very full of nerve, Miss Sedgwyck. I am not sure it is altogether healthy."

Caroline allowed the matter to die a quick death by retiring to bed. But another dispute was soon to follow.

The next morning, Caroline declared the weather too excellent to be confined indoors. She asked Edgar to order a carriage to be drawn for herself and the girls so that they could go to town. Perhaps they could buy a few items like trinkets, but nothing enormous, while seeing the sights. She did not think this overstepped her bounds, or that Lord Malliston, who was still away but had corresponded with Edgar briefly during his absence, would disapprove.

The girls were utterly delighted.

"We have never been to town to purchase anything," said Sophie.

One girl at each of her sides, both smiling in anticipation of their first trip to town together, Caroline found – much to her surprise, for Edgar was always reliable – that no carriage waited for them at the front of the manor.

"What is this, Edgar?" she asked him. He remained stationed at the front door behind them. "I distinctly remember standing here thirty minutes ago and asking that the barouche be drawn out for our trip to town."

Caroline had chosen the barouche in deference to the girls. It was her thought that they might be able to best enjoy the sights of Easingwold with the retractable roof. At the same time, should they become too timid under the eyes of the townsfolk, they could always pull the roof down again.

Edgar appeared to be blessing himself and muttering a prayer as if in preparation for some odious occurrence.

"Forgive me," the butler said. "You were gone not more than a moment, but Mrs. Humphrey appeared and announced that you had changed your mind and would no longer be in need of a carriage. This was not the case?"

Edgar, though, had a weary expression. He seemed to sense it was, indeed, not the case. At this, Caroline could only sigh. Determined not to be flustered, Caroline smiled reassuringly at the girls, and then at the butler.

"Mrs. Humphrey must have misconstrued something I had said."

The witch.

"Oh?" said Edgar. He knew better than to trust Mrs. Humphrey or her sister, Caroline was certain, but he would not want to cross either of them.

"I believe so. Would you be so kind as to see that the carriage is brought back, Edgar? The girls and I have dressed in our fineries. It will be such a shame to let it all go to waste, don't you think?"

Edgar went ashen. "You don't understand. Mrs. Humphrey had the carriage taken up for her own use. She and Miss Ball have gone to town. A few minutes ago, now."

Of all the nerve, thought Caroline.

She could see the look of disappointment on the girls' faces at this news, but she still remained unfazed.

"Then, we will simply have another carriage prepared," she said, knowing that the manor only boasted of two barouches. The duke had taken the other on his mysteriously long trip. "It truly will be a waste of fine clothes and fine weather if we were to be indoors all day."

"Of course, of course," said Edgar.

He was gazing at her in something akin to admiration. She had not spoken to the butler about the matter as she had Duckie, but the cook told Caroline that Edgar cared little for either sister and had, in fact, already been a member of the duke's household before his marriage.

Smartly, the old man called for one of the stable boys and sent him with word to the stables. The ladies had to wait only a short while before a carriage was drawn up before them. It was not the barouche, and the girls would have to sit close to the windows to gaze into the streets, but Caroline would not be deterred from their excursion by some old woman's petty trick.

Their expedition was every bit as gratifying as Caroline anticipated it would be. Phoebe in particular enjoyed the sights of people going about their business much more than Caroline expected. The little girl pointed and exclaimed at nearly everyone on Fleming Street selling and displaying their wares. For a reason known only to her, she was most taken by a man who was selling cast iron pans.

Sophie absolutely insisted that Caroline sit for a cheap portrait, and Caroline felt too happy to refute her. So she made a good bargain, arranged her skirts primly, and sat. After they arranged for the portrait to be brought back to The Thornlands, they proceeded to a sweetshop for some treats to reward the girls for their patient dispositions through the rather long course of drawing.

It would be neither an expensive nor thorough likeness, but Caroline was interested to see how it looked once it was finished.

They returned to a steaming, ready late luncheon and Duckie fussed over them, exclaiming delightedly at the pretty new hat that they bought for her.

"Oh my, Miss Sedgwyck, you shouldn't have bothered – not for old me," she said, though her smile was endearingly gratifying.

"Oh, you have the girls to thank for their thoughtfulness," said Caroline. "Phoebe was the one who mentioned that she would like us to bring you a souvenir of our expedition, and Sophie mentioned how your old hat got itself hinged on the door at mass last Sunday. She said it snagged dreadfully."

The cook beamed her gratitude at the little ones and gathered them in her large skirts for a hug. "You just made Duckie cry," she sniffed happily.

"Why are you crying, Mrs. Breem?" Phoebe asked in befuddlement, her voice muffled in the cook's thick skirts. "How could you cry and laugh both at the same time?"

At this innocent remark, the adult occupants of the room burst into laughter.

And it was in this happy mood that the Witch Sisters found Miss Sedgwyck, Phoebe, Sophie and Duckie. Miss Ball was the first to enter the room. Hearing the laughter, she paused at the doorway, causing her sister to crash into her. Bothered by this situation, Mrs. Humphrey regained her feet and promptly turned herself around the way she came.

Her sister, ever complacent, followed on her heels.

CAROLINE HAD WRITTEN to her father every week since she arrived at The Thornlands. In her missives, she elaborated on the many activities in which she had engaged herself. Above all, she wrote of her delightful wards – she spoke highly of Sophie's assertiveness and will of mind, and wrote paragraphs about Phoebe's sweetness and charm. She described the manor in grand details and related Duckie's kindnesses to her.

Only briefly did she mention the duke, and just to say he was away on private business almost invariably since her arrival at the manor.

She sought to reassure her father that all was well and, indeed, it was. But should she write a word about the positively bacchanalian gambling party, Father would be very much worried.

Heaven forbid she mention finding Lord Malliston in a compromising position outdoors in a garden.

In all likelihood, her father would then prevail upon her to return to York, lest her reputation be harmed while she remained under the duke's roof.

She knew that her father still hoped she would one day get married to a man worthy of her. Caroline had endeavored in all her capacity to discourage him from this notion. Marriage held little sway for her either way. But her father was stubborn; he would not budge on the desire. Caroline relented in her outspoken refusals over time, and her father dreamed that she might have a family of her own one day.

Now that she was in the employ of the Duke of Nidderdale, Caroline finally admitted that, despite not thinking much about becoming a wife, she had not made allowances for any event *other* than marriage removing her from her father.

She could not have known that for two engaging girls without a mother, she would be willing to change her plans. Once she realized this was the case, Caroline had no regrets about it. She did not tell Father that she would be happy carrying on this way for quite some time, but she did impress upon him how much she was enjoying her role.

The Witch Sisters were given no word of praise in Caroline's letters. Indeed, Caroline did not even discuss them. She saw little point in being so negative.

Her father's replies, in conjunction with her aunt's well wishes, always warmed Caroline's heart, until Arthur wrote in one of his letters, "Perhaps you might find a good recommendation from the duke to marry one of his friends." She knew he was not serious because, at best, she could expect to marry one of the duke's friend's staff. A valet, perhaps, or a steward.

In her next letter, Caroline made no effort to reply that should any of the duke's friends, such as they were, come near her, she might swoon in embarrassment at the indignity of such a proposal.

Instead, she commented on the mild weather and the beauty of The Thornlands.

Some things were much better left unsaid.

Still, she awaited the duke's return earnestly and could not fathom why she was being so silly. He was aloof, indisputably debased, and deeply troubled by his memories of war. The longer she had been here, the more obvious it became. Whereas her father withdrew into silence, she found that Lord Malliston was liable to explode. He was not loud or violent when displeased or troubled, like some other men, but he did have an unexpected core of steel.

Turning her pillow over to the cool side, she thought back to the day she had a few moments to herself and decided to play the pianoforte. She had never been very good, it was true, but it was still enjoyable.

The Witch Sisters were in town visiting with some friends, though Caroline found it a feat that they possessed friends among any of the people who knew them, and Sophie and Phoebe were napping. The duke was seeing to an errand and had been away from The Thornlands for several hours already. Given his past tendency to be absent for much longer than he vaguely said he would be, Caroline assumed she would have the house to herself well into the evening.

It was not to be, and she was shown the extent of the duke's temper. It was perhaps deeply buried beneath his aloofness, but it could flare unexpectedly.

She had just finished a simple song her father used to practice with his intermediate pupils.

It was only in the space between the final note and her next breath that she caught Lord Malliston's footfalls behind her. He strode into the room and she stood hastily.

Mentally, she cursed, thinking back to what the Witch Sisters told her about *never playing the pianoforte*. No doubt, Lord Malliston was not going to be pleased with her. Recalcitrant, she prepared her explanations. There was so little to do in The Thornlands that she must do something with herself or go mad.

They faced one another and she waited for him to speak first. He did not for some moments, simply staring at her, seething.

His mouth was pressed into a tight line, and rage lurked in his brown eyes. She could not help but note that sadness lingered there, too.

"Miss Sedgwyck," he said. "I was not given to understand that you were a musician."

"I am not, my lord," she replied evenly. "Not in the same manner as my father, at least."

"Yet, I did just hear music coming from this instrument, did I not?"

"You did."

He moved closer to her, and all Caroline could think of was a panther, not that she had ever seen one in the flesh. He was all coiled power, ready to strike. She still did not back down.

He said, with his body scant inches from hers and his face bent down to compensate for her stature, "It is *not* yours to play."

Stunned, Caroline said, "My lord, the house is empty except for the servants, Duckie, and Edgar, who have their duties... and the young ladies are taking a rest. I was simply—"

Lord Malliston cut her off. "Getting above yourself, I believe."

He was not shouting. He had simply raised his normally melodious voice. But he did not need to shout for the venom in his tone to be unmistakable.

Hurt, for she would never knowingly do such a thing, she tried again. "No—"

"Surely someone has told you that no one in this house *ever* plays the pianoforte."

She did not explain that Miss Ball and Mrs. Humphrey had done so. She searched his angular, handsome face, trying to understand why he was so incensed.

"It just sits here. Day after day, it would seem. Why on earth does it—"

He shook his head, giving a mirthless laugh. "Because, Miss Sedgwyck."

"Is it not better to play it once in a while? I am not an expert, but I assume that they need to be used or they degrade."

Lord Malliston's nostrils flared. "As I said, you are getting above yourself."

Feeling a stab of anger herself, she demanded, "Why? Because I am not as cowed as the rest of your household? My lord, Mrs. Humphrey and Miss Ball do not seem particularly deferential."

He brought back his fist and, for a fleeting instant, she thought he was going to strike her. She had never been hit by anyone in her life.

Flinching, Caroline waited for the impact.

But the duke pushed down his left sleeve and brandished his ruined hand in her face. "*This* is why," he said. She blinked and focused on the destroyed fingers, which had healed cleanly, but left nothing but meager stumps that ended before the first knuckle and were covered in scar tissue. "I cannot play, so neither can anyone else. You'll notice I have never mentioned either Sophie or Phoebe learning."

She wanted to protest, to say that was absurd, but she felt such an acute stab of empathy that she could not. Her fury deflated, and she could do nothing but look into his eyes and hope her own did not reveal too much pity.

He would hate that, she knew.

He moistened his lower lip with the tip of his tongue and let his hand fall back to his side. His gaze searched hers.

There was just a moment when Caroline foolishly thought they might kiss, but it passed.

He backed away from her with his eyes narrowed, and said, "*Never* play *my* pianoforte, again."

Although the words were uttered softly, they were laced with a sharp threat. Without even a backward glance, he quit the room and left her standing by the pianoforte with her heart beating hard in her chest. The insinuation was clear. He did not have to watch her for his order to be understood and abided by.

Father had never acted in such a way, but she could see that the same irrationality bred by combat and violence and loss drove both men.

No, thought Caroline. *Lord Malliston is a powder keg of ill thoughts, and instead of meeting them head on, he fetters his time away with bad habits.*

Her observations of and experiences with the duke had not, however, shifted her regrettable interests in him.

Though she would never admit it to anyone, she dreamed almost each night of being strewn over his lap in that overgrown garden. And when she awoke, it was with flushed cheeks, aching core, and a yearning heart, all of which she worked to calm before looking after her young charges.

Chapter Seven

"YOUR CHANCES OF winning at the tables today are worse than that of an old spinster getting a marriage proposal."

The gentlemen around the table laughed uproariously at their friend's comment. Reeve joined in the laughter, but his heart was not in it. He didn't take well to being teased and never had.

The speaker was none other than the Duke of Pierceton, Bellamy Bingham. He was Reeve's friend, but the good-looking rake would be nothing but pleased at Reeve's bad luck. He was his opponent on the gaming tables and had been winning Reeve's money all night.

Again, Reeve tossed the dice and threw up his hands in surrender when the odds went against him.

"I give up!" he groaned at last, his surrender giving way to another round of laughter from the spectators.

Bellamy gathered his winnings in his arms and grinned at his friend. "Blessed be the day I won against you in a game of dice!"

"Amen!" chorused many of the gentlemen about.

Reeve's reputation for luck was unblemished at the gaming tables. Until now, he had never found himself so soundly defeated. *It's a night of firsts*, he decided. Smiling only a little, he removed himself from his position at the table and went in the direction of the bar where libations were being served. *I need a drink.*

His three best friends and drinking partners, Jonathan Polk, Ashton Coldwell and the undefeated winner of the night's gambling activities,

Bingham, followed in his wake, stationing themselves all around him.

"You seem to have amassed all the luck as well as the winnings tonight, Bingham," he said without rancor as he grabbed a pitcher of ale.

His friend, however, was quick to disclaim any extraordinary stroke of fortune. "No, Reeve... at least, not where you are concerned," he said. "It is my opinion that I could only have won against you in one case. It seems as though your heart is somewhere other than in the games tonight."

"And there, Bellamy, are my thoughts exactly," announced Polk. He nodded sagely.

"Yes, I have seen an old bluestocking with a better hand at the tables," replied the Count of Aberdare, Ashton Coldwell.

"What ails you, my friend?" Bellamy slapped his shoulder. "It is the grandest crime to possess any troubles in my abode while I celebrate, and I must insist that you regale your friends with your woes immediately."

The others heartily agreed, looking into Reeve's face eagerly. All three were on their way to roaring drunk because they had been drinking and gambling all night. Only Reeve remained less drunk, for once in his life.

So they can teach an old dog new tricks, he thought.

All four gentlemen maintained a steady friendship based on their dubiously ethical leisure activities. Where one could be seen making merry, the others were not far behind. Titled, wealthy, and fairly young, the friends lived lives filled with leisure. They generally could not find it within themselves to care when society judged them harshly. Reeve was the single exception to that, but even he found that the fun outweighed the censure.

Tonight, it was a party at Salisbury Castle. Bellamy only recently came into his inheritance by virtue of his uncle, who had died without an heir. This announcement had been made most exuberantly at The

Thornlands, where Bellamy had arrived late as a consequence of the events leading to his exciting news. The new duke had explained that the deed of the title was entailed to go on to the next male in the family, and this was none other than himself.

Bellamy Bingham, to the dismay of the genteel members of the *ton*, had shunned all invitations to wait upon him now that he had come into his title. He knew already that mothers sought to exhibit their daughters before him.

Instead of enduring this socially acceptable manner of coming out with his new title and holdings, he had declared a fortnight of partying, gaming, and whoring for his closest of friends.

After the failed gathering at The Thornlands was relocated to one of Reeve's country houses in North Riding, the friends had all gone to Salisbury to celebrate with Bellamy.

At the moment, Reeve could only look into each of his friends' faces, frowning as he did. Unthinkingly, he blurted the first thing that preyed upon his mind.

"Do you not think that, perhaps, we might be in folly to be party-ing and gambling as we are? Have we any thoughts for the future as to the consequences of our actions? Could there... perhaps... be some repercussion in wait for us?"

Reeve, you are drunk.

His friends listened to him with the quietest of attentions, but when he ceased talking, there were expressions of utmost confusion on their handsome faces.

"We don't harm anyone," said Jonathan. He was not annoyed by Reeve's musing, but his dark features were shifted into a look of concern for his friend. "Why then should there be harm in wait for us?"

The others nodded their consent.

"We are not criminals hiding from the law, Reeve. We are titled lords, and we pay our duties," Bellamy added. "Why should we fear for the future?"

Reeve shook his head to express his frustration with his friends. He was certain that they would understand him in time, but they were all so inebriated. They would be unable to fully understand now. "Have you ever given a thought to getting married and having children of your own? What will happen to our lives... our parties... after you all settle down in matrimony?" he said, determined that they should somewhat see his line of thought.

Of the four, he was the only one who had ever been married. His friends had shown no particular interest in the process.

"Ah, Reeve, marriage is highly overrated. You always were the one to say that," said Ashton, after exchanging a nonplussed glance with Bellamy. He raked his fingers through his shock of ginger hair.

The count was right. Reeve's marriage had been a marriage of convenience, a strategy that he had carelessly and relentlessly pursued in order to come into his inheritance eight years ago. There had been no love between him and the daughter of his father's friend, William Devereux. Their marriage was only a means to an end.

His father, seeking to harmonize his family with Devereux's, had stipulated in his will that his dying wish was to see his only son married to his late friend's only daughter. There was also a financial motive underpinning this wish. Daisy Devereux's husband would also come into possession of the vast Devereux fortune and lands, and William, though untitled, was in possession of great wealth acquired through trade and farming.

Reeve had seen nothing wrong with fulfilling his father's wishes. He proceeded immediately to court and eventually wed the heiress.

A few months into the marriage, he started to wish he'd acted differently.

He would never have dreamed that Daisy was spoiled rotten, conceited, cunning, and selfish by design. But her true nature soon revealed itself. Her allies, the sisters Mrs. Humphrey and Miss Ball, manipulated her for their own gain and supported her schemes and plots. She proved to be uncommonly without regard for his welfare and took no responsibility for the household as the lady of the manor.

Her main concern was in emptying their coffers for expensive trinkets, attending balls wearing the latest fashions, and frequenting the theatre. Having children had done nothing to alter her disposition. Daisy would have nothing to do with her own daughters.

As soon as they were not within her body, thought Reeve bitterly, *she handed them off to the maids and the wet nurses.*

In the presence of his gentleman friends, Reeve had confessed many times that marriage was a lie, a trap that he had fallen into. Now, he found himself wondering if, with a woman other than Daisy, a woman who was perhaps more like Miss Sedgwyck, it could be different. The kind of idyllic, happy thing he used to contemplate as a young lad.

Hearing his words flung back at him so abruptly, Reeve could think of nothing to say that would convey his exact misgivings at the moment. He might have been the most sober of his friends, but that said very little. He was not actually sober at all.

"I believe that I am well acquainted with Reeve's woes," announced Jonathan, gathering the interest of his friends at once.

Reeve was delighted that somebody was taking him seriously when he himself didn't quite understand the melancholy that had befallen him. In anticipation of the revelation about to be disclosed, he gazed at Bellamy, then Jonathan, with a grin.

"Do you not observe that our fine friend here has not spoken to any of the girls from Madame Foxy's since we came to Salisbury?" said Jonathan.

Ashton and Bellamy both nodded heartily.

"Oh, I am in doubt of that, Jon," said Bellamy, teasing, with a twinkle of mischief in his blue eyes. "I saw this very pretty, dainty thing at The Thornlands the night I arrived, and I have never set my eyes on a lovelier woman. I thought she was one of the girls who had come to wait upon us but, alas, I gleaned nothing about her before our removal from the manor. Reeve, here, has been having a good time, I tell you!"

This newly revealed intelligence excited the gentlemen and they begged Bellamy to describe the lady in question in clearer terms.

Reeve anticipated it, too, for he had no idea what the duke was going on about.

Bellamy indulged their requests, describing a temptress with the fieriest hair, clearest skin, and brightest green eyes he had ever seen. He mentioned that they held such fierce, fearless mischief that he would not mind if she gazed at him all night.

Upon such a description, Reeve was quick to come to the realization that there was only one such person under his roof.

It was Miss Sedgwyck, the tutor who had so bluntly told him her thoughts not even three days into their acquaintance. He had thought over that afternoon often. He should have been more embarrassed that she caught him in such a delicate situation with one of the ladies, but all he could wonder was whether she'd been intrigued.

I daresay she was, he thought.

There had been anger in her expression, and mortification, too. She was young and probably rather sheltered due to her secluded life.

But the pink in her cheeks didn't just hint at righteous disgust.

Had she been wondering what it might be like to be in my lap? He shook his head. That sort of thinking would not do well for him. He was already troubled enough by the fact that Miss Sedgwyck was, as Bellamy had exclaimed, notably beautiful.

All she had done was berate him for the sake of Phoebe and Sophie, which she'd been right to do. That had edged out any potential curiosity on her part, hadn't it?

He had left The Thornlands, truth be told, because he was mortified himself. It was only in this moment that he understood exactly what had motivated him to make himself scarce.

He was not ashamed at having been caught out. He had done too many things like bed a woman in a garden to feel shame at just being seen.

He was ashamed at the thought of disappointing *her*.

With that rather alarming thought, Reeve knew that Miss Sedgwyck was responsible for his considerable melancholy in all the present time he had been away from the manor. His head beat painfully at this realization and, suddenly, he had no wish to drink another drop of ale.

How could he salvage this? She had made her opinion of him clear. From where she stood, he was nothing but the *Duke of Havoc*.

He had even told her never to play his pianoforte again, a show of temper that he could neither forgive himself nor apologize to her for. The cause did not matter. Such an uncouth display of emotion could not be explained away, and Reeve did not generally apologize for anything.

His friends were far removed from the thoughts wandering in his head, and they turned to him with curious eyes.

"Tell us, who is she? Have you gone and obtained a mistress for yourself now, Malliston?" asked Ashton.

Reeve was quick to disappoint them as he explained Miss Sedgwyck's presence under his roof. All three men made noises expressing their disillusionment, and the subject of discourse returned to the state of *Reeve's* present circumstances.

As he often did, Ashton claimed to be in possession of the solution to Reeve's ailment. Leering, he whistled one of the ladies over to their table.

"Reeve here will be in need of your genteel services all night long," said Ashton to the courtesan, much to the others' delight. "If you can get him to stay in bed well till tomorrow night, then consider yourself fortunate, for I shall reward you personally and most handsomely."

"Hear, hear!" called Bellamy and Jonathan, slapping their cups of ale against the table.

The lady of the night was immediately upon Reeve with a come-hither smile. She placed a hand against his chest and leaned closely toward him.

"The manner in which you address every concern is so characteristic, Ashton," Reeve said.

Like the reprobate he was, Ashton threw Reeve a jaunty salute. The others laughed as the woman pulled on Reeve's hand.

Reeve acknowledged that his friends would no sooner allow him to escape the situation than they would quit drinking. It was evident, too, that he would only be free of their teasing remarks when he was away from their company. Thus, Reeve allowed himself to be guided away by the lady.

Once above stairs in one of the many opulent guest bedrooms, Reeve removed himself from her grip and regarded her with grave eyes. Their surroundings were very fine, full of plush furnishings.

"You may take your leave now, Madam," he said, fishing for some money. "I have no wish for your companionship."

The woman was buxom, with long auburn hair that was let down all the way to her waist, and her dress was nothing but a sheer poppy red material that clung beautifully to her body, announcing her profession for all to see. Reeve guessed that she must be new in Madame Foxy's employ, for he had never seen her before. She was a beautiful woman of around thirty or so, but he found no excitement at her presence.

Hearing the firmness in his voice, she was quick to accept the payment and it quickly disappeared down her ample bosom.

"Thank you, my lord," she said, raising her eyes to his.

There was still an invitation to indulge in a long night of decadence, but the invitation was not all that Reeve saw within them. The color of this woman's eyes was a dark green with golden flecks.

It stunned Reeve into breathlessness and he almost changed his mind about bedding her until he was reminded again of the reason he did not want to avail himself of her pleasures, no matter how willingly they were offered.

The truth was that he had been challenged by a similarly beautiful woman. A woman with green eyes and the most intelligent of smiles.

He set about dismissing the lady as gently as he could, but for good measure, he locked the door after she had quit the room. Then, he sat upon the bed and, for the first time since he left The Thornlands, permitted his mind to wander in thought of the subject of his fascination.

His daughters' tutor was both intrepid and candid. Her courage was one he never witnessed in any female of his acquaintance.

Nobody, not even the self-righteous Mrs. Humphrey, had brought him to task over his parties. While Reeve knew with absolute certainty that his actions were not altogether exemplary for his daughters, he had never really considered that they might be impacted by them. That they might see or experience something untoward. They were still, to him, too young to notice anything at all.

Miss Sedgwyck had brought this error in judgement to his attention. Though he neglected to acknowledge the accuracy of her words and assessment of the situation, they had remained with him and prevented him from participating wholeheartedly in the party.

What was fascinating about her, however, was that she possessed this sense of ethics paired with an underlying interest in naughtiness. He was worldlier than she was and he could see the unspoken desire in her eyes. He understood it for what it was.

In a rare moment of self-reproach and candidness, Reeve agreed with Miss Sedgwyck that he was neglecting his daughters. He did not know if this was because of something the war had done to, or taken from, him. But he did know that it was supremely difficult to connect with them. To love them.

While she lived, he took perverse pleasure in accusing Lady Malliston of failing to care for her daughters. She *had* failed. But he had done no better after her death. While his battlefield injuries were perhaps a cause, he could not excuse his actions entirely. Sophie and even poor, shy Phoebe had both tried in their ways to draw him back, to involve him in their little lives, after he had returned home. After their mother had died.

Instead of letting them, he kept running off to the gambling tables and the arms of strange women.

I really may be the worst father, thought Reeve without any self-pity.

Reeve wondered how Miss Sedgwyck was faring with his daughters. He knew their welfare would be at the forefront of her mind.

He would do well to return home and see for himself, he decided.

Selfishly, he wondered if he could repair his standing in her regard.

Chapter Eight

I N THE DAYS following their expedition to town, Caroline was close
to overseeing The Thornlands herself, or as much as someone in
her position actually could, at any rate. This, of course, did not sit well
with the Witch Sisters.

It all started with the growing layer of dirt on the floors.

Caroline had noticed, the more acquainted she became with her
new home, that it was often – in a word – filthy. At first, before the
Witch Sisters had engaged her in an all-out war, she did not remark
upon the slovenly housekeeping. After all, it wasn't her manor.

Though she, Aunt Lydia, and her father were poor, their house
had always been clean. Knowing this, it was hard not to bring the state
of things to Mrs. Humphrey's attention. Originally, Caroline still felt it
was not her place to criticize the housekeeper.

As time went on, she did not give a fig about offending either sister.

The mantelpieces were laden with dust. The handrails were, too.
The wood flooring was scuffed. The marble floors had no sheen. The
curtains were as dusty as the mantels. The chamber pots were ghastly.

Caroline knew the small herd of house servants was not to blame.
No, as soon as the duke had disappeared, Mrs. Humphrey was content
to laze about, giving no direction to any of the servants who nonetheless valiantly tried to attend to their duties while lacking a reliable
overseer. Edgar, whose duty was not to be a housekeeper at all, did his

best to keep things in hand. However, he could only accomplish so much.

Exactly thirty days after Caroline had arrived, she and the girls were coming downstairs in anticipation of dinner. The happy trio had been in Caroline's room – Phoebe and Sophie were helping her compose a letter to her father.

The girls, who had never received letters from anybody, not even the duke, were always eager to read Caroline's post. They constantly begged to have their words written in her notes. Caroline saw no harm in indulging them.

It is good for them to practice letter writing, and who writes to them? Caroline thought, watching as they trundled down the stairs. Perhaps, she would ask her father if he could write specifically to the girls. It might ease some of his own loneliness.

"Sophie, mind the hem of your dress," she said. "It was just laundered." Sophie had been scuffing it along the ground, which was, as it perpetually seemed to be while the duke was gone, dusty.

Phoebe, who had become more outgoing in the last few weeks, trotted ahead of her sister and tutor. The maid had said it was her favorite dinner being served this evening: pottage, vegetables, and soup. As such, she was very keen on arriving to the table before everyone else. Caroline didn't have the heart to tell her that good manners would dictate she needed to wait to eat until all were served.

Suddenly, Phoebe slipped on the third to last stair.

Struggling not to curse, something she'd only done so much since beginning her employment with Lord Malliston, Caroline rushed forward and caught her before too much damage could be done. It would not have been a long fall, but Phoebe could have been quite hurt.

She was already so startled that she sobbed loudly in the way only small children could manage. It was an enormous sound from such a small being.

"Hush," said Caroline softly, as she scooped Phoebe into her arms. "It will be all right, Phoebe. I promise."

Sophie looked ready to cry, too, so Caroline allowed the girl to clutch at her skirt.

Still upset, Phoebe would not leave the sanctuary of Caroline's arms after they arrived in the dining room. Caroline scowled when Miss Ball and Mrs. Humphrey, already in their seats, hardly reacted to the crying child.

They could have been eyeing a cloud flitting across the blue sky for all they were concerned.

"My! Whatever happened to the child?" Duckie, roused from the kitchen, flew into the room as quickly as her short legs could carry her.

"She slipped on the stairs, I'm afraid," said Caroline.

With a frown, Duckie quit the room, but only after peering closely at Phoebe to ascertain whether she had been badly hurt.

The Witch Sisters merely offered icy platitudes that supplied no comfort.

"Do stop crying, Phoebe," said Miss Ball. "It would appear you have no injuries. You must cease sobbing this minute."

Caroline glared at her. "She's had a frightful scare, Miss Ball."

"We all agree that falling down the stairs could be perilous," said Mrs. Humphrey coldly. "But children must not be allowed to overplay their pain. It only cultivates an unseemly flair for theatrics and manipulation. Put her down, Miss Sedgwyck. She is only shedding crocodile tears."

Mrs. Humphrey's verdict was exactly what Caroline had come to expect from her. But before Caroline could reply cuttingly, Duckie blustered into the dining room again. Caroline almost held her breath.

She did not think she could negotiate between upset children and a massive argument waged by Duckie and the Witch Sisters.

"Well, she would not have to shed tears – crocodile or otherwise – if *you* had not failed in your responsibilities!"

Duckie, a good deal shorter than either of the spindly Witch Sisters, still glowered at them both fiercely.

Mrs. Humphrey turned imperious eyes upon her and rose from her seat.

"Whatever do you mean by such nonsense?"

"The poor child probably slipped on a layer of grime on the stairs – it wouldn't have been there if the scullery maids did their jobs as they should!"

"You fat cow," said Mrs. Humphrey with ice in her voice. "You cannot blame *me* for the ineptitude of servants or the clumsiness of a small child."

"Better a fat cow than a complacent housekeeper who can't direct her maids or *keep a bloody house!*" Duckie pointed a chubby finger at Mrs. Humphrey in nothing short of pure malediction.

Phoebe was starting to cry harder, while Sophie was again in danger of joining her sister.

"Enough!" Caroline said. "We shall proceed with dinner and we shall all converse pleasantly... with civility... or leave the room. Am I clear, ladies?"

Duckie is in the right, she thought. Gently, she set Phoebe on her feet and pushed her just slightly toward her chair. *But I doubt I can affirm her words without causing even more chaos.*

Mrs. Humphrey, Caroline could tell, would have contested this mandate, but perhaps because Phoebe was hiccupping dangerously, she held the peace. Duckie glared at the Witch Sisters but uttered, or shouted, nothing more to them.

"I do apologize, Miss Caroline," she said. Then, she began to serve dinner as though this was a normal, happy gathering. Her servings on Miss Ball and Mrs. Humphrey's plates were notably sloppy, but serve them, she did.

When dinner had concluded and she'd tucked the girls in bed, Caroline went in search of Mrs. Humphrey.

She found both Witch Sisters in the front parlor, sipping tea and muttering abuses against Lord Malliston, Duckie, Edgar, and Caroline.

Caroline ignored their looks of haughty guilt as she strode into the parlor and went straight to the heart of the matter. There was no call to be subtle.

"You will begin to take your duties seriously, Mrs. Humphrey, or at least give me leave to instruct the servants to do theirs. I worry for the girls' safety. And what will Lord Malliston say when he returns and sees how things have deteriorated?"

In due course, after they had been digested, her words were met with indignant protests from each woman.

"You are quite ridiculous, Miss Sedgwyck," said Miss Ball, her expression caught between supreme dislike and amazement.

"Hardly," said Caroline. She directed her next statements at Mrs. Humphrey. "If the duke discovered that Phoebe nearly injured herself due to bad housekeeping – and you cannot deny that the accumulated dust and dirt make everything quite slippery – he would dismiss you without hesitation."

I don't know if that is strictly true, she thought. *But it sounds sufficiently serious.*

"Have you taken leave of your senses?" asked Mrs. Humphrey. She arched one thin, incredulous eyebrow. "What makes you believe he would take your word over ours?"

"He does not have to – at least, he won't have to if things around the manor do not improve. Why, he could be the next person to slip on something."

Caroline wished she knew when he was going to make his return. All of this was beyond her and for some reason known only to her heart but not to her head, she missed him. How silly it was to miss a man she neither seemed to like, nor knew well enough to hold in high esteem in the first place.

She watched as the Witch Sisters seemed to think on the idea of

Lord Malliston suffering injury within his own manor when even the fields of Salamanca had not killed him.

Miss Ball shrugged. "The duke is quite nimble. His hearing suffered, not his gait."

"Is that a jest, Miss Ball?" asked Caroline suspiciously.

It had to have been, because Mrs. Humphrey had to hide a snicker with a cough. This drove Caroline to consider harsher measures.

While the Witch Sisters exchanged amused glances, she said quietly, "I believe Lord Malliston has told all the household never to paddle Sophie or Phoebe." She ran a finger along the mantelpiece. Unsurprisingly, it came away brown. "However, I have it from both girls that each of you has, in fact, gone against his express wishes."

With deliberate slowness, she looked from the tip of her finger to the sisters. The unguarded looks on their faces were enough to confirm that the duke's daughters were not telling fibs. Their reluctance to speak meant the Witch Sisters had paddled the girls, indeed.

Caroline began to smile. Just as the grandfather clock above the mantelpiece struck ten, she said, "I take it I have your permission to give instructions to the servants, then."

Without further ado, she stepped out of the parlor.

In the room behind her, the stunned Witch Sisters sat in their chairs with their tea growing cold.

THE DUKE ARRIVED home one cold morning, just when Caroline started to fret that he might not return soon at a time when he was sorely needed.

Only a few days prior, the girls started to ask after their father and trudged about the manor with long faces, entreating her to make him come back to them.

"Did Papa leave because we were bad, Miss Caroline?" Phoebe had asked.

Sophie then told her sister, without waiting for Caroline to make any remarks, "Papa runs away because he thinks we are too much trouble. At least he does come back."

She uttered it with little self-pity, but hearing those solemn, adult words in Sophie's girlish voice made Caroline's stomach lurch.

"No, Phoebe," said Caroline. "Papa leaves because he is troubled and he likes to distract himself."

It was the simplest and most truthful way she could deflect the girls' self-blame.

But their despondency only increased Caroline's vexation with Lord Malliston. After that exchange between Sophie and Phoebe, she told Edgar to notify her immediately when the duke returned.

Edgar had opened and closed his mouth several times like a fish but, finally, he nodded and said, "Yes, Miss Caroline."

So when one of the maids, a young lady called Alice recalled Caroline, roused her at six in the morning, she conjectured that Edgar had done well by her and Lord Malliston was home.

Sleepily, she asked Alice, "Has Lord Malliston returned?"

Alice said, "Yes, Miss Caroline."

"Did he send you to me, or…"

"Yes, Miss. Edgar informed the duke that you wished to see him."

And he has not delayed in seeing me, thought Caroline. She sat up, willing her heartbeat to slow down. He was a careless, callous man. He did not deserve such anticipation.

He left his daughters alone in this enormous house with no one but the Witch Sisters, the cook, and their tutor for company for weeks, she told herself. But she said, "Thank you, Alice. Where is the duke now?"

"In his library."

Alice left with a curtsy. Sighing deeply, Caroline rose. She went to her wardrobe, deliberating over what to wear for the day. She should not have cared at all what she wore to converse with Lord Malliston, but she chose her best dress, the lilac one that had so worried her the first night she ate dinner with the girls. In less than fifteen minutes, she was dressed and presentable.

Why was she bothering to be punctual when he had demonstrated a distinct inability to attend anyone but himself?

"I am glad that you have returned to The Thornlands, my lord," she said to him without preamble, as soon as she entered the library. He was standing on the other side of his desk, nursing a steaming cup of tea and gazing out of an enormous window that overlooked the vast, but somewhat stark, gardens.

She had rehearsed several speeches on her way through the manor, the inhabitants of which were only just beginning to stir, yet *that* was all she could manage. Pathetic.

"As am I," he said.

He appeared very well. *His eyes are such a wonderful, warm brown in this lighting*, thought Caroline. Perhaps it was all of the library's wood panels casting their color onto his countenance, in conjunction with the early morning light.

Immediately following the complimentary observation, she chided herself.

Stop that.

Caroline also noted that he looked the slightest bit drawn. She attributed it to his journey, and what had most likely been days on end of nefarious activities.

At the moment, he was staring directly into her face as though trying to memorize her features. She felt it was a little strange but, for all she knew, he had entirely forgotten how she looked. If, indeed, he had ever noticed in the first place.

"Tell me, how have my daughters fared?"

"I must say that they would be a delight for any tutor," she said warily. There was much she wanted to discuss with him. "They simply soak up knowledge."

Is this all he wants to know about his children?

"I wonder if they got that quality from me. Their mother was not fond of learning because she was not very good at it," he said, reflecting. Then he smiled a little. "I retained facts quite well. Although I must say I squandered the ability. I neglected my schooling, preferring instead to dream of glory found in far-off lands. Well." He trailed his left palm along the edge of his desk. "You see where it landed me. But you must have excelled as a tutor for, before your arrival, they were incredibly disinterested in their lessons."

Caroline bit her lip. "There may be more reason for that than my academic prowess, my lord."

He frowned. "What do you mean?" Then, as though recalling what sort of polite behavior was expected of the lord of a manor house, he asked her, "It is still early. Forgive me. Do you require tea?"

Stricken, Caroline blinked. "Ah…"

"Do sit, Miss Sedgwyck, and I shall have Alice bring you some."

She sat, mutely observing as Lord Malliston walked past her, and she could not help but think what a fine figure he cut in his more casual traveling clothes. He stuck his head out into the corridor to hail down a passing servant, a young boy whose mother worked in the kitchens.

She heard the duke quite clearly and evenly state that Alice was to be sent here, upstairs to the library, with some morning refreshments for Miss Sedgwyck.

It was the first time she had heard him be anything less than gruff with a servant. What had happened to the man?

"My lord?"

He returned to his space behind the magnificent desk and sat in his own chair. "Yes?"

"As I was saying… the reason why the girls may have been so reluctant to learn their lessons before now?" He nodded, and she plunged forward into the worst of it. "They…" she shook her head, disgusted.

"What topic is so awful that your usual bluntness has been clipped?" asked Lord Malliston. "Before I left, you were comfortable haranguing me in my own garden when I was not even properly attired."

His eyes glowed with humor and Caroline blushed.

She resolved to look anywhere but at him. She was thinking, yet again, of what it might feel like to be seated on his lap.

"I believe that they *have* been paddled by the Wi –" she caught herself before she could say *Witch Sisters*. He might appreciate the name but, then again, he was tempestuous. "By Miss Ball and Mrs. Humphrey."

The duke went murderously silent.

"I am sorry, my lord. I did not know until the girls told me… or, rather, neglected to tell me."

He leaned across the desk toward her and, suddenly, she had an idea of what he might have looked like while on the battlefield. "I know what their antics can be like. Those *bitches*."

Caroline gave a short gasp, but she did not disagree with the word.

He chuckled wanly. "My apologies, Miss Sedgwyck. I forget myself. But I can only imagine what they have put *you* through these last few weeks. The manor is in near shambles." So, he had noticed the poor housekeeping that Caroline, with Duckie and Edgar's help, had only recently been able to combat. "I can also only imagine that you took every opportunity you could to shield the girls from the sisters."

She thought to deny it, then nodded, instead.

"I wish I could say I did not believe you and that I trust they would abide by my rule. You are new here. They have been with me for some years, now. Yet I don't trust them," he said flatly. "I have given direct orders that the girls should never be paddled, and yet…" he broke off, still leaning quite close to Caroline. "They *would* do it if they wished and had the opportunity."

"The girls are quite terrified of them, and I can think of no other reason why they might be," said Caroline. "To be brutally frank, my lord, they often unsettle *me* and I am a grown woman." She did not feel much sympathy for Lord Malliston's predicament. In a low voice, she muttered, forgetting herself, "But at any rate, they would have plenty of opportunities to abuse Sophie and Phoebe without your knowledge. You are always gone. And the girls are almost as terrified of you as they are of the sisters."

As soon as the words left her lips she regretted them, if only because she might lose her position. *Well*, she thought, *what's been said has been said.* She wondered if she would ever learn in her lifetime to be more circumspect, and what it was about this man that drew blunt speech from her more readily than a local landlord drew ale from a keg for his regular patrons.

But she had forgotten the duke's awful hearing.

He peered at her warily and it was clear that he had not understood exactly what she had uttered. Her disapproving tone and expression, however, must have been unmistakable, for the beginning of anger was rising in his face.

Not for the first time, she wished she knew if he could read lips. She did not believe so.

"I beg your pardon, Miss Sedgwyck? You will need to speak up, I'm afraid."

Caroline cleared her throat and said loudly, more forcefully, "My lord, I was making the point that if either sister wished to paddle the girls without you ever finding out, it would be easy to do since you are rarely here long enough to have proper conversations with your daughters," she said. She took a long, steadying breath. "And unfortunately, they are almost as scared of you as they are of Miss Ball and Mrs. Humphrey. For different reasons, to be sure. They long for your approval and are convinced they do not have it."

She met his eyes and knew instantly that she had gone too far. *In for a penny, in for a pound*, she thought. "I do not feel in my heart of hearts that Sophie or especially Phoebe would tell you if she had been paddled. They did not even tell *me*, in as many words."

"Do I understand correctly that you seem to blame me for my daughters' mistreatment at the hands of these shrews?"

She sighed. "Yes." Her voice was barely above a whisper. "Somewhat."

"Speak up, Miss Sedgwyck," said Lord Malliston. He wore a sharp grin.

"I do," she said, her cheeks flaming. She purposefully spoke in a loud staccato. "From an outsider's perspective, it seems as though there is much you could do to prevent this situation, yet you refuse to do it."

Perhaps I am being too harsh, she thought.

The duke was so close to her that she read not only fury but also dismay in his countenance. She studied him for the dreadful moments he kept his silence. It appeared that he had a habit of remaining quiet after she spoke to him, and she did not know if that was because of some effect she had upon him, or if it was his usual way of conversing with anyone. She had never seen him socialize with respectable members of the *ton* in his home. From what she knew of the aristocracy, his manner was out of the ordinary.

Given the state of The Thornlands, it was better that he did not receive visitors.

It probably contributes a great deal to his gruffness. Social graces are a disused skill for him. And no matter how charming, it would be hard for any man to counteract all of those ghastly rumors. Not everyone is so rational as Father.

Almost a minute passed while he said nothing and she fought the impulse to squirm. He was not classically handsome in the way the heroines of novels seemed to prefer in the men they idolized.

His features were too sharp and leonine for it, but he was *engaging*, Caroline decided.

"You are overstepping your remit, Miss Sedgwyck," said Lord

Malliston, snapping her out of her reverie. "It is not for you to judge my actions!"

"Or lack thereof," grumbled Caroline. "That is the problem, my lord, not your actions themselves. You appear to act very little when it comes to your family."

"I do not think I want to have heard your comments, that time," he said. "But would you be so bold as to repeat them for the sake of a damaged man?"

"You do not act when it comes to your girls," said Caroline with clarity. "That is the problem!"

Lord Malliston was shocked. "Actually, Miss Sedgwyck, in the future, I would heartily prefer not to hear it when you make such pronouncements." He leaned onto his elbows, using the desk for support. He stared at her as though she were an utterly alien creature brought up from the depths of the ocean. While he was in this position, they were eye-to-eye, and Caroline devoutly tried to maintain her composure. She was equally exasperated and captivated. "Thank you for putting my blunted hearing into perspective," he said acridly.

It was then that she realized she, a common woman with neither title nor connections, had wounded him.

How? she internally questioned. *Was it what I said? The reminder of his shortcomings with his daughters? Or of his impairment? At least when he was angry that I played the pianoforte, I knew exactly what I had done to cause offense.*

Softening, she said, "My lord, I am sorry if I offended you." She consciously did not say, "If I hurt you."

"And I am sorry if I goaded you."

That surprised her. "It must not be pleasant to be reminded of one's inability," she replied carefully. "Besides, I am told that I have a rather cutting temper." She offered him a small smile.

"You have a quick wit," said he. "It seems to join forces with your temper. I do not know if I would consider it to be a *disproportional* temper, however."

"I will consider my words more carefully in the future, and also try to speak more clearly."

"For my part, Miss Sedgwyck, I shall listen better, and not allow my pride to flare," he said. "You are correct... my daughters are rather nervous around me. It does not help anything, and I *am* their father. It is entirely my fault. I have not been raising them in the manner that young titled ladies should be. I have even relaxed many matters of decorum since my late lady wife's passing."

"Such as?" Caroline was too ignorant of the finer points of society to notice.

"Well, the use of their titles, for one. Technically, they should be addressed as *Lady* Sophie and *Lady* Phoebe. I suppose I will need to amend that before long but, fortunately, due to my own reputation, they have not been around other children of their status. They do not know it is not quite the done thing to always be called by their given names."

"I see. That makes sense, because my father is always careful to use his students' titles if they have them... until he wins them over, which he almost always does. Then they are too comfortable with him to stand on ceremony," she said fondly.

"Arthur was a refreshingly unassuming and warm man when I knew him. He is unconventional, but I could not imagine many young people being uncomfortable with him."

Emboldened by the girls' misfortune and the opportunity to help change it, as well as, to some measure, the duke's physical closeness and kinder words, Caroline said, "May I ask, my lord... why are the sisters still in your employ?"

She felt it was safe enough to inquire, as their abrupt spat seemed to be behind them.

Lord Malliston sighed and rubbed his temples, causing some of his brown hair to fall forward. She itched to touch it.

"Because, Miss Sedgwyck, Lady Malliston made me promise that they always would be."

Caroline accepted this explanation, letting it seep through her mind. She better understood the Witch Sisters' arrogance as well as their complacency.

She could barely believe it in light of his behavior, but his short, simple answer made the most sense. He was only trying to keep his promise to a dead woman as a widower should.

Carefully, she considered the issue. That was all well and good, but it seemed to her that the time had passed to honor the agreement.

He must have more integrity than I gave him credit for, or else he would not mind breaking his word.

Alice broke the silence, entering the library after a respectful knock at the door. Since there was no table save the one near the fireplace, which was opposite the duke's desk and across the large, stately room, she simply set the tea tray on the desk itself.

Lord Malliston eased back into his chair, surveying Caroline seriously.

"Might I propose an idea, my lord?"

"Please do," he said as Alice poured Caroline her tea. There were even buns for her to eat.

"I have studied the sisters' characters, trying time and time again to find something redeemable about them. But they have no sense of affection for the girls. Nor do they have any respect, it would seem, for you."

She waited to see how the duke would respond to this. When he only gave her the slightest of droll smirks, his eyes crinkling at the corners, she continued.

"While my suggestion may seem cruel and might offend your sense of responsibility to your late lady wife, I think you should let Mrs. Humphrey and Miss Ball go." She paused and took a sip of tea.

Alice slipped by Caroline just in time to hear this, but the expression on her face was unreadable.

"Do you?" said Lord Malliston. He was quite calm.

This calmness confused Caroline, given he'd just shown his considerable temper not a quarter hour past, but she swallowed and carried on.

"If I had the influence, I would insist upon it. Think of Phoebe and Sophie, my lord. They are miserable with the sisters here in residence. You would not need to be cruel. It is possible that you could serve Miss Ball and Mrs. Humphrey their notice, yet still help them find new positions." Daringly, she added, "Not that they deserve such consideration. And ideally those positions would be well away from any children."

Lord Malliston gave a hearty bark of laughter. "Very well. But how do propose this might be done?" When she wavered, he prodded, "Go on, then."

"Well, one way could be to settle them in your country homes as housekeepers. I imagine that with reasonable compensation, they would be content to spend the rest of their days being as lazy there as they are here, but without the consequence of driving us all mad or the girls to nervous fits."

Stubbornly, she took a bite of one of the buns so she would not have to speak for a few moments.

Eventually, and much to her relief, he grinned. "What an elegant solution."

"Thank you, my lord," she said. "So... you will see the sisters resettled?"

"Yes. Without delay, I should think. They've done enough wickedness in their time here."

Caroline studied him as covertly as she could. There was one more topic she wanted to raise with him. Although he had responded far better than she hoped to her proposal regarding the Witch Sisters, she knew that Phoebe and Sophie could provoke him unduly.

This, she suspected, had most to do with his feelings of inadequacy as a father. What else would make such a competent man so surly? Surely, this was the root of many of his problems. The neglect of his daughters... his inability to keep control over the chaos in the manor...

She drank a little more tea to steel her nerves, trying to decide what to say.

But Lord Malliston resumed the conversation for her.

"You have something else you would like to discuss, Miss Sedgwyck," he said.

Irritably, she thought, *Good gracious, can he just see inside my head?*

"Yes, my lord."

"Go ahead. You have been invaluable, thus far."

There was that disconcerting note of amusement, again.

"I daresay that I have grown attached to Sophie and Phoebe, and they to me," she began stoutly. "Because of this, they are very frank when we are alone. While you were away, not at first, but as time went on, they began to ask where you were. Then they began to blame themselves for your absence."

Lord Malliston went very still.

"My lord, it is not my position to take you to task for your life-style," said Caroline. "But I am afraid that your daughters do not regard themselves as well as they should because they believe they have failed Papa. They feel that you leave when they have been naughty, or when you cannot stand them." She fixed him with a pleading gaze.

The duke became very interested in the tea tray. Presently, he said, "May I have a bun, Miss Sedgwyck?"

"You do not have to ask, Lord Malliston," she said hurriedly, wondering if he was ignoring everything she had just said, or if some war injury that affected his mind was finally making itself known and he was becoming distracted.

She nudged the tray closer to him and, with his marred hand, he took the last bun.

"You must think me very wicked," he said after he had taken a few small bites. Even his small bites were large; there was scarcely half a bun left.

Perhaps in some ways.

"No... I think... well, it isn't for me to say."

"How could you believe I'm anything but? My behavior has not contradicted the rumors you must have been aware of before you came, for one thing." He shook his head. "All I can say is that I am appalled that my own daughters believe they are the cause of my... restlessness."

Slowly, Caroline said, "They are young and their minds are very impressionable. I am sure that they would not want to hurt you with their words. But they... they just want their father. Do you understand?" She tilted her head. "I believe that if you were home at The Thornlands more often and made an effort to spend some of your leisure time with them, it would go a very long way. The damage is not permanent."

He was quiet as she spoke, staring at her from across the desk. Caroline had no means of knowing what he thought of her advice. All she could do was continue to sit and wait for his response. Her tea had gone rather tepid, but she drank it anyway.

"Very well." There was a strange hoarseness to his voice that Caroline had never heard before and she wondered at its cause. She did not quite think that he was about to cry, but it was encouraging that their discussion of his girls' feelings about Papa had roused his emotions. "Yet again, you have been very frank with me. You are correct." With a reluctant smile, he repeated, *"Again."*

His acquiescence was all that Caroline could wish for and, in truth, his smirks and smiles were starting to go to her head in the same way brandy did. She had never been truly drunk, but she felt as though she had imbibed a few fingers' worth. Her limbs were warm and her mind was starting to retrace its familiar dangerous paths.

She wanted to find the girls. They must have been at breakfast, by now.

"Thank you for listening, my lord."

He held up his right hand as though to quiet her. "You could have ignored everything you have ever brought to my attention and still received your pay. Some of the things you have said might have earned you your notice from another employer," he said. "But I should likely be thanking *you*." His smile broadened.

Even she, in all of her inexperience with men, could not mistake the warmth in his next words or the appraising glint in his eyes while he said them.

"It seems Mr. Arthur Sedgwyck sent me an angel guised as a tutor."

Chapter Nine

FOLLOWING THE DUKE'S return, many shifts began at The Thornlands.

The most notable was the departure of Mrs. Humphrey and Miss Ball to another of Lord Malliston's country houses outside Matlock in Derbyshire.

True to his word, he had firmly told the women to avail themselves of his kindness. Otherwise, he'd said, they could always return to their families as burdens without positions.

They chose the former option. With the Witch Sisters gone, all the other occupants of the manor breathed a collective sigh of relief. Phoebe and Sophie were so exuberant during the sisters' departure that Caroline felt obligated to tell them not to be so rude while Miss Ball and Mrs. Humphrey could still observe them.

Of course, secretly, she shared in their joy.

The next change was more of a shock to her.

At his steward's behest, Lord Malliston was summoned to oversee some matters of estate. He had only been back at The Thornlands for a fortnight when the summons arrived, and he promised to be gone only about a week. Neither Sophie nor Phoebe fully believed him, but they dutifully nodded and kept from any shows of crying, which they knew he patently hated.

It was only the middle of the week, and Caroline and the girls were engaged in reading through a French primer. She had their full attention. Phoebe, in particular, seemed to love learning the foreign language. The weather outside was foul. Thus, they were using the back parlor – freshly cleaned and rearranged – to conduct their studies. Gradually, she realized that the girls were no longer paying attention to the words on the page.

Finding this odd because the girls had never let their attentions stray during lessons, she glanced up to see what captured their interest. A short gasp escaped her lips.

"My lord," she said. "I had no idea of your return. What has brought you back so soon?"

Lord Malliston stood in the doorway, staring into the room with such hesitant longing on his face that Caroline was sure she misread it. His clothes were damp and rumpled from travel.

Has he come directly from the carriage? And how long has he been standing there?

His daughters regarded him warily. They, too, were surprised. He had never once bothered to see them at their lessons, and he certainly had never returned home *early* from an excursion.

"Nothing of concern," he said. "I just wanted to see Sophie and Phoebe, and so... here I am." He took long strides into the room and although his boots left mud on the carpets, Caroline would not stop him. She beamed at him and, for some reason, this made him falter, but he carried on toward the girls. Though still shocked, they jumped from their chairs and went directly to him.

"Papa!" exclaimed Sophie.

The duke enfolded his daughters in a cautious embrace. He was unaccustomed to showing fatherly affection, but he was trying. Caroline smiled to see how the children clung to his trousers. She, too, rose.

"Welcome back, my lord."

"Ah... my thanks, Miss Sedgwyck."

"We must resume our lessons, young ladies," she said, by way of rescuing the duke.

"Papa only just returned," said Phoebe. It was the first time she had ever voiced an issue with any of Caroline's directives.

"And so, you must allow him to wash," she said.

She smiled at Phoebe, who pouted a little, but did not raise another protest.

"Miss Sedgwyck is right," said the duke. "I must go for now, but I'll return if she permits it."

Caroline gave her leave, and the girls finally, albeit reluctantly, released their hold on Lord Malliston's dirty trousers.

Scarcely an hour went by before he came back to the parlor. Much to Sophie and Phoebe's delight, he sat with them for the remainder of the lesson, unobtrusively listening and saying nothing. Briefly, Caroline wondered if they should switch to anything but French, arithmetic, even, but he did not seem to mind it being spoken around him.

The same thing occurred the next day, and the day after that.

At dinner on Friday, for as it happened, as well as frequenting lessons, he had also been taking dinner with Caroline and the girls, he suggested that the family go for a Saturday picnic in town. The girls were beside themselves with joy. Caroline was both surprised and pleased by his suggestion.

Then Phoebe demanded of her father, "Papa, may Miss Caroline come, too?"

Lord Malliston looked from his daughter to her tutor and grinned. "It would be my pleasure."

Caroline, who had been quickly planning a somewhat lonesome afternoon, blushed at his expression. *He does need someone to mind the girls*, she thought. It was really the most practical arrangement. He was not yet used to looking after both of them.

So it was that, together, they sat in the park watching the passersby while eating a cold luncheon that Duckie had packed for them.

Almost everyone peered at them in surprise, and Caroline realized that most of the people of Easingwold must still know the Duke of Nidderdale by sight. He did not spare them a glance, and encouraged his daughters to do the same. Caroline was slightly more bothered than her charges or their father. She supposed that she, unlike anyone of the *ton*, was simply not used to being the subject of such obvious and garish speculation.

But it worked. With morbid curiosity being unrewarded by either a spectacle or hysterics, people soon left them to their own devices. After some time had passed, the girls wanted to engage their father in a run.

He will say no, thought Caroline. She readied herself for the girls' tears.

They were not to come.

The duke said to Sophie, who had suggested the race, "You do know, Daughter, that my ability to *run* has not been at all compromised." He raised his eyebrows at her.

"I still think I, at least, could best you," she said.

Phoebe was less certain, but seemed to be willing to run against Papa and Sophie.

"Then, let us see who is the better runner."

The three of them took off at a fast pace, but Lord Malliston soon lagged behind his daughters, glancing behind him with a fond look at Caroline. Sophie and Phoebe made it several yards away from him before they realized they had won, and were gleeful in their victory.

When the group departed the park near sundown, they were all pleasantly tired. The day, however, threatened to turn sour upon their return to The Thornlands.

After a short respite, during which Caroline attended to the girls, changing them from their mussed day dresses to frocks more suitable for dinner, and changed her own attire, they joined Lord Malliston in the drawing room.

Quite innocently, Phoebe asked, "Papa, would you please play for us before dinner?" She nodded to the pianoforte.

"Yes, Papa, do – you never play," said Sophie. "Miss Caroline probably doesn't even know you can!"

A dreadful silence fell across the room as the duke gazed helplessly at his daughters for a moment. Caroline soon deduced that, in all their innocence, somehow the girls did not understand – or had never noticed, given his extensive absences from their short lives – their father's wounded left hand.

Caroline recollected Mrs. Humphrey's words about the duke and the pianoforte, and grudgingly acknowledged that there was truth in at least one of her statements. *I need to say something to distract them*, she thought desperately. But she was afraid of adding coal to the fire, so to speak. He had made such solid progress that she did not want to make him feel angry or nervous in front of his daughters.

The duke was quick to recover, though. With a smile, he gathered his daughters into his arms and settled them on one of the deep blue sofas. "Perhaps you recall how Papa went to war with the Duke of Wellington?" he said.

The girls nodded eagerly, anticipating a story-telling episode.

Caroline kept silent and lingered near the fireplace.

"Aye, I did. While in battle, a huge fire exploded where I stood… and this is what happened." He glanced at Caroline first, and then he showed them the hand with two fingers missing. He let Sophie gently touch the nubs that had once been digits. "I have not tried to hide it from you, but I have not told you the specifics, either."

Caroline closed her eyes for a brief moment. She knew that the *huge fire* was really a cannonball. Shrapnel had cost him his passion for music.

Her young wards were, as ever, quick of mind.

"Papa cannot play the piano anymore," said Phoebe sadly.

Sophie asked, "Did the fire burn your ears, too, Papa?"

The duke sighed. "It did. The explosion was so loud, I became nearly deaf."

"I am sorry, Papa." Phoebe began to cry. "I shall try to speak louder to you."

Sophie clung to him as she, too, started to sob quietly. "The Duke of Wellington is a bad man," she declared.

"No, my sweet, you must not think so," said Lord Malliston. He gazed at Caroline in desperation.

She came closer to the sofa to rescue him. "Remember our lessons about political affairs?" she asked, as she gently placed her palms on each girl's back. Their heads bobbed. The lessons about politics had been as simple as Caroline could make them, but she had tried to help the girls understand the realities of war and diplomacy. They had often asked about it.

"Everyone, including your papa, owes the Crown and England allegiance. Bad people constantly try to destroy our way of life, so we must fight to stop them. Every man has to respond to a call to arms unless he is too young, or too old, or too ill. Like my father, your papa only went to defend us. He is a hero."

Her words appeared to soothe the distraught girls. Their sobs soon waned and they looked more thoughtful about their father's recent past. She only hoped they would not badger him to *try* to play.

"Miss Sedgwyck, would you be so kind as to play in my stead?"

Lord Malliston's question shook her. She glanced at him as though she was the one who could not hear properly. "My lord?"

He had made the request in earnest and his mouth was half-upturned in a smile. Phoebe looked up at her curiously, and Sophie said, "Do you play, Miss Caroline? If you do, you have not taught us."

"I do not play well, Sophie," she demurred. "I would rather teach you a variety of other things. When you are a little older, perhaps Papa will find you a wonderful music tutor. You can learn to play *and* dance." She had not inherited her father's nearly perfect ear or his love of music. What she *had* inherited was her mother's keen mind alongside Arthur's auburn hair, and the latter only meant she was often teased as a child.

"I am sure you play adequately," said Lord Malliston. He was teasing her, now, but it was warm and good-natured. "How could you not? I did not have the chance to hear Arthur play anything, but I did hear him sing. Such a rich voice."

Caroline did not want to bring up the incident involving the pianoforte with the girls present.

But tactfully, she said, "My lord, I am sure you remember our discussion about who was to play this instrument." He met her eyes in understanding. "And who was not. I was given to believe I was not."

"So you *do* play!" exclaimed Phoebe. "Papa, she should play."

"Yes, Phoebe, she should," he agreed. "But I regret to say that I forgot my manners with Miss Caroline one day when she'd first come here."

Is he really going to own his mistakes in front of them? Caroline thought.

She was impressed. But the duke had changed almost immeasurably, lately. She conjectured that he had started to return to the way he was in his youth, possibly even before his marriage.

She did not know for sure, but the way he spoke about Lady Malliston, or did not speak about her, led her to believe he was not necessarily thrilled with the match. She did not think about it overmuch, because she found that the very idea of him having been married to another woman provoked an animal sort of jealousy with which she was unfamiliar. But she could imagine a younger Lord Malliston in his late teens, perhaps just come into his majority, with the same dry humor and warmth as this older Lord Malliston.

Sophie was indignant. "Papa, why? Why would you not be polite to Miss Caroline? She is always polite, herself!"

Caroline had to disguise a smile by clearing her throat. She certainly was not always polite where Lord Malliston was concerned. "I had not asked permission to play the pianoforte."

"Oh," said Phoebe solemnly.

She had recently been learning how important it was to ask permission before using others' possessions. Caroline wanted to break her of the habit of "borrowing" Sophie's dolls without asking.

"I suppose, Sophie, that it has a little to do with the war, too," said the duke. "Like my hand and my ears, you could say that it also hurt my mind."

This was a very large concept for two young souls to grasp, but they tried. Caroline watched them try to make sense of it. Phoebe's face screwed up in concentration and Sophie frowned.

"But you can still speak and do sums and I know you look after the manor, and the houses in the country," Sophie insisted.

Caroline let Lord Malliston explain further in his own way, and in his own time.

"I know, pet, and even that is lucky. Some men cannot manage those things after they return," he said patiently. "I guess I mean to say that it hurt my emotions."

Impressed indeed, now, Caroline thought, *I hardly recognize the man.*

"Is that why you always go away?" asked Phoebe. She had made the connection between Lord Malliston's fraught mental state and his inability to remain content at home, however tenuously.

"Yes, darling, in general, that is why I have not always been here."

"Was it harder to stay after Mama died?" Sophie looked up at her father with enormous blue eyes.

Lord Malliston hesitated. "It did not make things any easier," he said. Then he steered their conversation back to its original point. "But because of things that have happened to me, both abroad and at home, including Mama's passing, I do not always keep my temper the way a good man should. I lost it with Miss Sedgwyck."

The girls looked at each other and a silent agreement passed between them. They knew how strange his impulses and responses could be, even if they did not know what had shaped them.

"My lord, you had every right to take me to task. None of this is my personal property," said Caroline.

Of course, she did not appreciate his sharp response to finding her at the pianoforte, but she at least linked the outburst with his horrible past experiences rather than taking it personally.

"No," he said firmly. "You are part of my household and you are not a servant. I should not have overreacted. It was ungallant of me, and uncalled for."

"But you must terribly miss playing. If I could no longer read or write, I would be miserable."

"I do, indeed. Very much so. But that is no excuse for my behavior."

Satisfied and touched by his admission, she nodded. "Thank you, my lord."

He smiled slowly and broadly. "Now, will you please play? Someone wise once told me that instruments need to be played or they will fall into disrepair." He winked.

She chose a carefree ditty that she was sure Lord Malliston and, perhaps, even the girls had heard – by the time she struck the second verse, warbling along as best she could, all matters of missing fingers and lost hearing appeared to be forgotten.

The duke sang, too, and at least his voice had not suffered.

It was, in truth, mellow and warm and deep.

This whole incident and the previous weeks' events forced Caroline to consider whether her early, forthright censure of him had done any good.

She dared to hope it had. The man before her bore little resemblance to the stiff, cool employer she had first met upon arriving at The Thornlands. Neither did she see the rake who left his family at a moment's notice to take his place in the gambling dens of York or London, or who had the audacity to hold outrageous whoring parties within the same walls as his own children's bedroom.

Perhaps Lord Malliston *was* a changed man.

Chapter Ten

FOR THE FIRST time in the dark months that had followed the battle of Salamanca, Reeve outright refused an invitation to a party. In all, he was pleased with himself. It was high time he began acting in accordance with his family's needs and not just his own selfish whims. Selfishly, though, he did hope that Miss Sedgwyck would notice and approve of his abstinence.

But his friends, thinking he had not received the missive at all, came immediately to call upon him at The Thornlands. As it transpired, they seemed to blame the footman dispatched to deliver Reeve's invitation.

Jonathan, Bellamy, and Ashton had settled in the drawing room, delighting in Duckie's delicious fruit scones and slurping tea as they awaited their friend.

"Servants are becoming quite addled these days," said Ashton.

"It will all be remedied soon enough," answered Jonathan complacently. "Reeve is never one to miss a party."

Reeve walked into the room without waiting for Edgar to announce him and, immediately, the three bucks began to explain why they had come.

"Reeve, you cannot imagine! We sent Ashton's footman with a note for you," said Bellamy. He was dressed as impeccably as always, despite his apparent agitation. He ran a hand through his blonde hair. "But the fool must have lost the letter, falsified a reply written *by you*, and delivered it to us. The nerve! I would have him dismissed if he was in my employ."

I should have known it would come to this, Reeve thought. He couldn't help but be a little amused at their slight frenzy. *It would never occur to them that I would refuse an invitation.*

He patiently waited until their laughter abated before he gave his shocking reply. It would be shocking to them, at any rate.

"No, the footman found me," he said. "I did write a reply saying that I would be unable to make the party."

The silence that followed his words was, Reeve noted, actually comical.

Bellamy's jaw slackened enough to allow a slight amount of spittle to pass from the corner of his mouth. Ashton's hazel eyes nearly crossed with surprise, and Jonathan seemed momentarily unable to comprehend human speech.

However, Jonathan was the first to speak.

"*You* sent that note in response to our invitation?" he asked incredulously.

"Yes, Jon," the duke said, quite complacently.

"What jest is this, Reeve?" asked Jonathan.

"No jest. I am deadly serious," said Reeve. "My daughters need me at this time, and I am unable to leave them in pursuit of my pleasures." He paused. "Were I to leave, it would make me both selfish and negligent."

"But your daughters have done exceedingly well as of late – you have said so!" Bellamy's voice rose in both volume and pitch. His friends always remembered to speak very loudly around Reeve, but this was almost more of an outright shout.

"No," said Reeve. He pinched the bridge of his nose. "I was never telling you the truth. It was easier to lie. You do not have children and would not understand." He felt as though he was betraying his friends, but he was not about to change his mind. "I have been sorely neglectful of them since my return from Salamanca, and even more so since Lady Malliston's death."

None of the three could say anything sensible in response to such a candid revelation. Each stared at him, mixed emotions playing on their faces. There was some resentment, a little anger, but largely, confusion.

Finally, Jonathan drawled, "Lord have mercy on us all – Reeve Malliston, the *Duke of Havoc*, just chose his daughters over us. I never thought I'd see the day. The end of times is truly upon us."

"As well he should," said Ashton. There was actually admiration in his eyes as he looked at Reeve. "He may have a point."

"Does this have anything to do with the delectable *tutor* I happened upon?" asked Bellamy. His expression was shrewd and calculating. Reeve could almost hear the cogs working in his mind.

He gave the question some thought before providing an answer. He knew that if he spoke as forwardly as he would like to, he would never hear the end of it. He also knew that if he lied, they would all see right through it.

"Perhaps."

"There always is a woman involved," sighed Bellamy.

The others echoed this sentiment with grumbles and sighs, but Ashton was, by far, the least scathing.

"Regardless, I feel I am a changed man," Reeve said.

"How changed?" said Jonathan, brushing scone crumbs from his jacket. "You will regret this more enlightened decision. I am sure of it. You will become bored and go mad."

Regret not spending the nights with strange women? Regret not losing more of my money to Bellamy? Regret failing to alienate my own kin?

"No, I daresay I won't," said Reeve mildly. "Just so that I am clear, you are all still most welcome in my home whenever you wish, despite any changes I have made for myself. You are also entirely welcome to finish your tea. Duckie would hate to hear her scones had gone to waste." He surveyed the small storm of a mess they had already made in his drawing room. Bits of scone littered the luxurious rug and the saucers had, thankfully, caught dribbles of strong tea before they could reach the table. "But I'm afraid I have matters to attend to. Therefore, I will be unable to entertain you today."

It was Ashton who shepherded the others back to the sofa so that they could finish their refreshments, even despite their marked disappointment in Reeve.

Reeve thanked him with a silent look of gratitude.

One of them, at least, understood, or was trying to understand, his shift in priorities.

REEVE WAS NOT arrogant enough to believe he had changed entirely or that he could make no more improvements. But, he was astute enough to recognize and acknowledge changes for the better when he saw them. It had been one of his better qualities as an officer. Though he was demanding, he also knew when to praise a soldier. He also knew when to praise himself.

No, he had a longer way to go before he or anyone else would deem him "respectable". Changes on their own did not make habits and he needed to prove he had better habits. He *was* spending more time with his daughters and, by default, Miss Sedgwyck. But he was making up for, in Sophie and Phoebe's case, years of neglect. Those could not be undone in a matter of mere weeks.

And as for Miss Sedgwyck. Well, she intoxicated him.

They had developed a steady friendship built on growing trust and warming regard. He fancied that she was starting to respect him as much as he respected her. It was not easy to tell for sure, for she was not easy to read when it came to more womanly emotions. But her manner toward him had softened even though her frankness had not changed. It was one of the qualities he liked best about her.

He also cared about whether or not she respected him, which was a new and disconcerting feeling. He had gone months without a care for what others thought of him.

This was, of course, a learned behavior. He likened it to calluses or muscle memory. He could teach himself to think differently and to care more, but it would take time.

At the start of his fall from societal grace, he had worried very much about his reputation. Eventually, he stopped worrying. It was easier.

As he was about to mount the stairs, leaving behind the crestfallen trio in the drawing room, Reeve spied a liveried servant on horseback making his way toward the manor. He turned back to the foyer and exchanged a puzzled look with Edgar, who was passing through and had also witnessed the approach from one of the wide front windows.

"It's quite a day for visitors, is it not, Edgar?" Reeve said wryly.

Edgar gave him a toothy smile. "Indeed, my lord. Though I over-heard you sorely disappoint your friends."

The butler obviously approved.

Reeve replied with a smirk, "You have become worse than Duckie. Eavesdropping never appealed to you before."

Together, they waited for the servant to approach the great front doors. Edgar received him promptly and ushered him toward Reeve.

"My lord," said the servant, giving a smart bow. "I come with an invitation to a private ball in York, at the house of Lord Poppleton and his wife, Lady Anne."

Reeve's first inclination was to scribble a negative response to the invitation. He turned it over in his hands thoughtfully, eyeing the pristine script.

Then, his mind wandered to Miss Sedgwyck's lovely green eyes and he began to smile. What would she look like in the finest dress meant to stun onlookers? It would be unorthodox, taking his daughters' tutor to a ball.

But he was the very definition of the word "unorthodox". There was no denying it. No doubt, Lord Poppleton and his lady wife would have an apoplexy when their servant delivered the *Duke of Havoc's* positive reply. They were quite old, if he remembered correctly. He might actually kill them by accident.

Reeve finally went up the stairs, beaming from ear to ear with impish glee.

He needed to ask a lady to accompany him to a ball.

❧

GROWING UP, CAROLINE had often imagined herself attending a ball. It had colored many of her fantasies.

Nonetheless, she almost immediately regretted telling the duke she would go to the ball in York with *him*.

What on earth possessed you? He is not courting you; he is your employer and, just barely, your friend!

Girlish fantasies had long been replaced by reality. Life had not presented her with opportunities to attend any fine parties or balls as a guest. The only time she ever had, it was in the company of her father who was hired to play the piano, and that was five years past, now. Only sixteen, she had lingered in the corners trying not to attract much attention. Really, she ought not to have been there at all, but Arthur did not have the heart to deny her.

He would be the first to say that Caroline could dance like any lady of the *bon ton*. She had enjoyed dancing since she was a young girl and she had an aptitude for it. They had spent many a merry evening with Aunt Lydia taking up the role of a male participant and Arthur playing song after song so that Lydia and Caroline could dance. But that was not at all equivalent to a real ball with rules and dance cards and sniping gossip.

Though she had never told her father, it was one of the only ways she could get him to play for his own enjoyment after he came home. When he played for her and Aunt Lydia, he was almost the way he had been before the horrors of battle. If Arthur thought he was helping Caroline, he gladly resumed his place at the piano.

Despite the fact that she knew she would at least be able to dance as well as any other lady, her nerves were nearly shattered when the fated evening arrived.

She kept sneaking glances at Lord Malliston while they rode in the carriage to York. They were on their way to a respectable inn. Really, it was closer to a hotel. He sat across from her, eyeing the passing scenery through the glass.

"My lord?"

"Mm?"

"You don't suppose too many people will…" she sighed. "Gossip."

About us, she wanted to say.

"People always gossip, Miss Sedgwyck," he replied. She would have sworn he smirked at her.

Shaking her head, she glanced out of her window, too.

"My lord?" she tried again.

"Miss Sedgwyck."

"I have never been to a ball."

"I should think not."

She did not ask him why he was taking *her*. Instead, she said, "I do not understand enough about society to do you credit."

He looked at her with faint amusement and said, "You don't value yourself well enough. Your manners are impeccable when you choose to use them, and I don't know if this would be of any comfort to another woman, but no one knows you. You may remain a wallflower if you wish."

"That is not strictly true, is it?"

"How do you mean?"

"Everyone knows *you*. By proxy, that means they will wish to

132

know who I am. I'm certain I will have to behave very specifically, or risk doing great damage to my own reputation. And yours, if by accepting this invitation you wished to begin rebuilding your standing in society," said Caroline, willing him to accept her urgency.

"Astute as ever," sighed the duke.

"I cannot mention I am your daughters' tutor, can I?"

She did not want to imagine the floodgates of censure and sniping that would open should *that* knowledge be made public.

"You are a former comrade's daughter, and a friend of my family."

Caroline gawked at him. "You mean to insinuate we are of the same *station*?"

"Well, when I introduce you, I shan't give you a title you don't have, but I will not act as though you are beneath me in any way," he said. "A ball isn't necessarily always for the gentry alone, and besides, you are my guest. I was invited, ergo you are invited."

He said it with finality and a slight haughtiness that belied his up-bringing. This was not a man who was told "no".

"Fine, but is there anyone that I should… especially show respect?"

"Customarily, the hosts. In this case, they are elderly and fairly jovial. They will find you charming. Lady Anne likes to wag her tongue about everything and everyone, but that has always been the case. Just remember to be circumspect." He beamed at her. "Lord Poppleton is very hard of hearing. More so than me, I would wager. Speak very loudly to him. You may need to shout. I expect he's only become worse in the last few years I have not seen him."

Caroline bit her lower lip, thinking. "And is there anyone I should avoid?"

"It's difficult to predict who, exactly, will be in attendance, but if I notice anyone who concerns me, I will point them out. In general, any groups of young males are to be avoided."

He suddenly looked quite fierce. "I would not expect you to know firsthand. But they tend to be uncivilized *en masse*, and more so if they are inebriated."

Caroline did not mistake his meaning. She nodded once.

"You are far too clever to fall prey to them but, unfortunately, balls can be their hunting grounds."

He would know, she thought.

She had heard enough gossip even in her tiny corner of the empire to glean how dangerous entitled men could be to a woman. Her dear friend Georgiana's cousin, who lived in Bath, attended a public ball some years back and was cornered in a garden by an opportunistic lieutenant on leave.

She shuddered, thinking of the consequences for poor Lucy's future. Caroline tried not to recall her overmuch, but she had been utterly disgraced through little fault of her own.

While Caroline might have risked ruining her own reputation in a completely different manner by hitting a reprobate upside the head or bloodying his nose if she could manage it, fearful Lucy did not consider refusal to be an option.

Lord Malliston watched her closely as her mind flitted through these unsavory remembrances. "I see I *didn't* have to warn you about *that.*"

"No, my lord. I fear that women who share my circumstances in life are unduly used by such men." She did not elaborate.

It's hardly very appropriate conversation.

He leaned toward her and asked very seriously, "Do you trust me?"

"I believe I do, yes."

"Then know that I will keep you from harm should the unhappy occasion arise."

She believed him.

THERE WAS A little confusion when Lord Malliston inquired about their rooms at the front desk. Although the clerk was perfectly polite in tone, he still raised his eyebrows when he asked, "You and your companion, my lord, will be in separate chambers this evening?"

Unruffled, the duke said, "Yes. We shall, indeed."

He smiled pleasantly at the clerk until the young, spotty man grew red around the ears and groped for two sets of keys behind the desk, all the while refusing to meet the duke's eyes.

Caroline, however, could have died of mortification on the spot. She had been all but named as a woman of the night, and the duke had done nothing to correct the clerk. She prayed silently that the separate rooms might signify the propriety of their arrangement.

Her traitorous mind, on the other hand, wished that she and Lord Malliston *could* share a room. It would have been scandalous and there was no way she could do so without shaming herself or her family name. Still, she wanted it.

But ever since the duke had started to make improvements upon his personal character, she found herself even more irresistibly drawn to him. Before, she was not innocent enough to pretend her thoughts about him were chaste. But now, she also dwelled upon his character, which was proving to be steadfast, if a little fanciful, and his dry, quiet humor.

It was a dangerous combination. Although her earlier attraction had been physical, it was now more than that alone.

As though they really were friends, they had started to retire together to the drawing room after dinner, after the girls had been tucked into bed. The venue was not strictly traditional and as a respectable woman, she should have sought her repose in a parlor. Caroline would also play the pianoforte for him. Soon enough, she discovered that he loved literature, politics, and the sciences as well as music, and they rarely ran out of topics to discuss.

Sometimes, she went to bed hoarse of voice because the volume at which she needed to speak to him was rather loud, but she did not mind.

Perhaps, their growing closeness had led to him inviting her to Lord Poppleton's ball. He did not have to go and, indeed, the duke who had first hired her probably would not have gone.

But this new Lord Malliston seemed to be more interested in social graces.

She only wished that he would give more care to how *she* might be perceived under such circumstances. He was used to being the subject of derision and speculation, but she was not, and she knew without a doubt that the ball's genteel attendants would talk exceedingly about her.

Caroline could no longer deceive herself.

She was fully taken with Lord Malliston and she could not fathom a solution to such a problem.

Therefore, she was even more worried that the *ton* would pick up on her infatuation.

What if I am too transparent? They will be cruel, and they will be quick to be cruel.

It was the stuff of gossipmongers' dreams: a young, unknown lady infatuated with an aristocrat. She might be forever labeled as an upstart or an opportunist.

Even as she readied herself for the ball, all alone in her room with the exception of a lady's maid sent up by the innkeeper, she found that she was almost beside herself with anxiety.

Duckie, Sophie, and Phoebe had masterminded her beautiful ensemble. She herself had very little to do with it. They had accompanied her on a rushed visit to an esteemed modiste in town with the duke's assurances that he would take care of all the expenses. The thought that he was paying drove Caroline to fearful indecision, but the girls and the jolly cook had all but taken over for her.

Her dress was ivory white silk with delicate lace trims at the hemline, sleeves and neck. The sleeves were capped at her shoulders, and she had long, kid leather gloves that reached her elbows.

The square neckline swooped low along her bosom, which caused Caroline no small measure of unease. She had never worn such a dress. But the ladies who worked in the shop, their mistress, and Duckie had assured her that the cut was still within the parameters of decency.

It was, they each declared in their ways, the height of fashion for young ladies.

She was left with no choice but to purchase the expensive, beautiful piece of clothing, as well as a pair of new satin slippers for dancing. Even Sophie and Phoebe had gone into raptures when they saw how Caroline looked in her new finery.

They, she thought, *were not at all scandalized.* It gave her some consolation. But then, they had been taken with the ladies of the night who had been invited to The Thornlands.

Caroline smiled her thanks at the maid, who was weaving her long curls into a braid, and wrapping the braid into a bun pinned at the nape of her neck. *I don't want to be too ostentatious.* She knew the shade of her hair already drew its share of attention.

She wore no jewels, and simply completed her evening attire with a butter yellow pelisse embroidered with delicate flowers and butterflies and a white reticule.

Looking in the mirror, she decided that she was as unadorned as she could be while still appearing elegant enough for a ball. Scarcely anyone could accuse her of greedy motives now.

How wrong she was.

Her first indication otherwise was the duke's unabashed surprise as she approached their waiting carriage at the front of the inn. He stared at her for so long that she said lightly, trying to lessen her nerves, "You look as though you would rather not go to the ball with me."

"No," said the duke, as though he was being roused from a dream. "I shall have to spend my entire night beating off your admirers with my bare hands, and wouldn't *that* be fodder for the gossip mills."

She couldn't hide her smile at his pronouncement, and she allowed him to help her into the carriage. His hand was wonderfully warm in hers, despite the fact that both of them wore their formal gloves.

Caroline believed that was it not for his infamous reputation, she would be the one fighting off *his* admirers. Not that she had much right to, other than currently being his guest to the ball. She kept the thought to herself.

"I must warn you about something," Lord Malliston said, just as they started to move.

"What would that be?" said Caroline, although she did have some idea of what he was about to say.

"I asked you to come with me to this ball because I wanted to have your company. I greatly value it," he said. "But that was, perhaps, selfish. You may be subjected to rather unkind talk."

She laughed a little. "That is the only thing that has worried me."

Not the only thing, but the primary thing.

He smiled at her admission. "In truth, I cannot blame anyone for their suppositions. I did not do enough to ingratiate myself after I returned from Salamanca and it hasn't even been a year since Lady Malliston has passed." He sighed and looked directly at Caroline, who basked in the gaze of those brown eyes. "Yet, without any warning to anybody, here I am, turning up to a ball with another woman."

Caroline asked the question she had once been so impatient to ask.

"Please do not answer if you think I am being impertinent. But how, exactly, did she die?"

She no longer believed he was a murderer. But she still had to know the circumstances of Lady Malliston's death.

Long moments passed before Lord Malliston cleared his throat. He leaned toward her, resting his forearms on the tops of his thighs.

"I was the only one who witnessed it," he said.

"The only one who *witnessed* it?"

He nodded. "I know that sounds strange. But it was not illness that took her. While I was away, Daisy began to take some suspicious medications... opiates of different classes... until they drove her mad. Mrs. Humphrey claimed that she had abused them because she loved and missed me too much, but we never boasted a loving union. I think she simply became reliant on the medicine, as one can. It is why I did not use it, myself, even though I could have. Our marriage was one of convenience, you see, so I did not ever believe the sisters' insistence that their mistress went mad for wont of me."

Caroline hoped she did not exhibit too much pity. Lord Malliston would not appreciate it. "I did not realize."

"I am more inclined to think she missed our quarrels because she was irrationally inclined to argue needlessly." He chuckled without any mirth. "In any event, upon my return, I found she could no longer recognize her own children. I was also a total stranger to her. She did not know me, such was her stupor."

The duke had the air of someone confessing a long-buried tale. Caroline's stomach dropped.

"The first night we spent together, again, I awoke to find her with a knife at my throat, screaming that I was a stranger."

"I..." Caroline was at a loss. *What an awful, awful thing.*

"I would not have heard her, had she not been screaming. My hearing had not yet returned to even the sorry state it is in, now. Everything was muffled and indistinct. Quite frankly, it was a terrifying experience."

Caroline never imagined there was such a grotesque story behind Lady Malliston's death. She had come to think, until Lord Malliston said otherwise, that illness was what claimed his wife. There was stark sadness in his eyes as he related the tale. She was overcome by the urge to take his left hand in her right, and so she did. He did not disengage her.

"I overpowered her, and she appeared subdued... normal, even.

She apologized. But I still had Edgar send for the apothecary. I didn't know what could be done, but I felt that, perhaps, she might benefit from some philter or elixir. I have seen men go mad in the military, Miss Sedgwyck. I've even known them to become dependent on drink or insidious medicines."

Woefully, he squeezed Caroline's hand.

"But before any help could arrive, Lady Malliston ingested some concoction. Something that poisoned her veins." He winced. "I had no idea anything like that was so available to her. It could have been a concentration of her medicine, or something else. We never found out for certain."

Speechless, Caroline could only cling to his hand in horror.

"I couldn't save her," he said softly. "I only left her for the briefest moment to fetch us some water and brandy. That was as good as if I held the poison to her lips and forced her to take it. I watched her convulse, and weaken, and ultimately die. Miss Ball and Mrs. Humphrey did not see what happened, but they heard at least the end of it. Duckie was away visiting her brother's family. Edgar was engaged waiting for the apothecary."

"No, that is ridiculous!" said Caroline, shaken from her rapt silence.

"What is?"

"You must not blame yourself."

"It is rather hard not to, unfortunately. We did not like each other, it is true, but we had a family together and I was the final person to see her alive. I will always wonder if she was secretly miserable despite everything I could give her."

"You cannot think that way," Caroline said. "How would you have known? How was it your fault? Your self-blame is... admirable, in some ways... but pointless. And inaccurate. You married because your father wished it, and women so often have little say in who they marry." She reflected. "Though, I now better understand many of your past inclinations. You were not just a hedonist. You were burying your emotions."

Having said her piece, Caroline looked into the night as their carriage moved through the streets, passing houses with brightly lit windows.

"I believe you have a penchant for being right when you express your opinions, Miss Sedgwyck," the duke observed after a while. He squeezed her hand.

"My father always grumbles about it."

"As to the matter of the speculations that are sure to arise at the ball... if we give out as little information as possible, I believe that will put off the gossipmongers."

"Or it will exacerbate what they say," said Caroline. She gripped his hand very tightly out of fear. She then realized that it was his left hand, and his glove had been very cleverly crafted to give the appearance that the hand itself was normal. When one put pressure on the stiff middle fingers that were not actually real fingers, they gave slightly in a manner that true flesh and bone would not.

"I prefer to let them say what they desire. They always do, in any case. If they cannot find out much about you, then they will return their tongues to the topic of Lady Malliston." He sighed. "They cannot do her any more harm in death."

"Was there ever any legal basis to the rumors that you were her murderer?"

"There was, of course, an inquest as a matter of formality. But the magistrate cleared me of all suspicions and charges. It did not stop the public from calling me a murderer, thanks to the poisonous mouths of Miss Ball and Mrs. Humphrey."

Although she did not agree with his choice in tactic and would far rather have confronted every gossiper of her own accord, she shrugged and said, "You would know more about combatting gossip than me. Unfortunately for your sake."

That garnered her a smile.

She was learning to prize his smiles.

Lord Malliston looked at their hands, which were still joined. Though he straightened back in his seat, he did not let her go. Instead, he stroked her palm with his thumb. "I believe something like this," and he indicated their hands with raised eyebrows, "would only fan the flames of new, eager rumors."

She smiled back at him when he still did not relinquish his grip.

✦

MANY WONDERED AT the duke coming to a ball at all, and with a woman in tow, no less – one so young and beautiful, at that. Others simply wanted to know what kind of a woman it was who had brought the *Duke of Havoc* out of his dark manor. She had flaming hair and the delicate features of a temptress, but she did not carry herself like one.

Reeve was ready for the gentle murmur that greeted their announced arrival. He knew instantly that Caroline, though she was brave, was not. He muttered in her ear with a smile, "Courage," before walking to a footman with a tray full of glittering glasses of punch. He did not go far and she did not meander away from where he left her.

A full two minutes had not passed before he heard a reasonably familiar voice at his elbow. It spoke loudly and confidently.

"Who is that delicious slip of a thing you've brought with you, Malliston?"

Bristling, he looked into a pair of hard blue eyes. It took him a moment to recall the man's name and title. This was, or had been, a friend of Bellamy's until they had a falling out over some woman they were both courting.

Lord Cuff. Reeve finally settled on his name.

"She is a family acquaintance," he said neutrally. He did not wish to give much away about Miss Sedgwyck, though it had been unavoidable to volunteer her name. "And how have you fared, lately, Cuff?" Reeve neither cared nor wanted to know, but still he asked.

It was a pointed change of subject, and Cuff would have none of it.

His broad face arranged itself into a calculating grin, nearly a leer. "She looks too fresh to be one of these cosseted young ladies." Cuff looked around exaggeratedly at the highborn women who populated the ball, all of whom, it was true, carried themselves as though they had always been going to balls and dances. They each wore more jewels, had more curls in their hair.

By contrast, Miss Sedgwyck was almost too austere, though she was glowingly beautiful. Reeve felt that she was perfect as she was. If she was too adorned, the jewelry and complex accoutrements would only compete with her vivid natural coloring.

Accepting two glasses of punch from the footman when they arrived at the front of the small queue of guests waiting for refreshments, Reeve said simply, "She is not cosseted."

Cuff took a glass for himself and sipped. Then he stroked his lower lip, thoughtfully. "You say she's a friend of the family, but be honest with me, Malliston. You have not been seen with a new woman since your wife's death, and you've quite the reputation for being popular with the *ladies*." He emphasized "ladies" in a telling way to establish that he was not speaking about the particular ladies before them. "She's a commoner, isn't she?"

"I hardly see how that matters."

"Well, it doesn't, exactly," said Cuff, as he arched an eyebrow. "I'm just trying to understand how I might find myself taking your delectable friend to a ball."

Outraged, Reeve opened his mouth only to be cut across.

"Do you know who she reminds me of? My little sister had a music teacher with a redheaded daughter. Obviously he never brought her to the manor, but I saw her once or twice walking to meet him after he'd finished his lessons. From the state of their dress, and judging by the fact that they walked instead of taking a carriage, I took them to be upon hard times." Cuff looked gleeful. "Sedgwyck, I believe their surname was."

Reeve shut his mouth, but his heart was in his throat.

"Is this her profession, now? I can hardly fathom how one aging man would be able to provide for both of them. Come on, Malliston."

"She is not a..."

Reeve was so livid he could hardly string together words.

"I've got to attend Lord Acton's ball in a few weeks and I would bet that with a few little additions to her wardrobe, I could get her to pass as one of us." Cuff was staring at Miss Sedgwyck lasciviously. "It would get Lady Acton off my scent. Married women who want liaisons are so tiresome, don't you agree? She has been after me for weeks and weeks. It's frightfully boring." He took a deep drink of his punch and licked his lower lip. "I'd not mind sampling this Miss Sedgwyck's wares, myself, though. Are they any good, old man?"

Cursing the ice that seemed to have encased him, Reeve tried to respond.

"Too right, the volume at which I'd have to discuss that with *you* would mark us both as incurably debauched. This isn't the time or the place. I'll call on you sometime soon, though, so that I may have the details to procure her services."

Not if I throttle you, first, thought Reeve. He pawed reflexively at his cravat. Regrettably, that was also exactly what he said aloud to Cuff.

The cad was so shocked that he backed away from Reeve, staring at him as though he had just sprouted an extra head in the middle of their conversation.

THEIR HOSTS, LORD Poppleton and Lady Anne, were lively octogenari-
ans, gracious, but as curious as the rest of their guests. They tried most
doggedly to ascertain Caroline's relationship to Lord Malliston.

"Have I seen you at court before, dear girl?" asked Lady Anne,
who was tiny of stature, yet formidable in bearing and so laden with
jewels that Caroline feared she might tip over at any moment.

Caroline smiled at the stark curiosity in her bright, grey eyes. "No,
ma'am, you must not have," she said, providing no more detail.

"Your surname is Sedgwyck, you said?"

"Yes, Lady Anne."

"I do not know of the name, personally."

"I would be very surprised if you did, my lady, for the name is not
so illustrious," said Caroline, watching with concealed amusement as
the old woman's confusion and intrigue both increased.

In the end, frustrated, Lady Anne left Caroline to her own devices
and went in search of other unsuspecting prey who might yield more
pleasing tidbits.

Lord Malliston appeared calm and unruffled when next they met
to dance, and they exchanged stories of those who tried to gain
intelligence about them. Caroline remembered one man he spoke to
for some time near the punch, and asked him, "Was the man you were
speaking with when we first arrived a friend? I saw you both looking
over at me and couldn't divine what you were talking about, especially
since you said we should not encourage gossip by supplying details."

That caused Lord Malliston to look considerably less calm. "Lord
Cuff," he said with a sneer. "And he is not a friend."

Wisely, Caroline let the subject die.

Although he evidently came to fisticuffs with no one that she witnessed, he danced most of the dances with her in an attempt to save
her from the many men who wanted to do the same.

By the time the night was dwindling to a close, the whole venue
was alive with talk of the lady with surprising beauty and poise who

had captured the *Duke of Havoc's* cold heart.

Who was she? She was not of the *ton* for she bore no title that she had specified, yet she did not have ill bearing.

Surely, she was not a doxy. Lady Anne herself gave her own opinion most decidedly on that idea.

Why did the duke seem to be so changed? Did the mysterious young woman understand the rumors about him, or was she simple in some way?

Everyone, from Lady Anne to Lord Poppleton, was simply longing to know more about Miss Caroline Sedgwyck.

⁌⁂⁍

THEIR JOURNEY BACK to the inn was punctuated by comfortable silences and laughter over how obvious the *ton* could be when its denizens wanted to know something about anyone. Caroline hardly wanted the carriage ride to be over because she knew that when they arrived, they would go to their separate rooms and the spell of companionship would be broken.

All too soon, they were getting out of the carriage, Lord Malliston first. He helped Caroline down with a smile. "Thank you for a lovely evening, Miss Sedgwyck."

"I should be thanking you, my lord," she said, shivering a little in the chill.

It was quite late, and although Lord Poppleton had offered them accommodations, both Caroline and Lord Malliston preferred more seclusion than would be granted in the Poppletons' household. Lord Malliston had explained in the carriage once they had departed that they would be expected to join their hosts, and any other guests who had lingered overnight, at breakfast. Caroline had wholeheartedly agreed that the inn was, by far, the preferable option.

"Then let us share a mutual thankfulness," he said, his eyes twinkling. "And go inside, for it's become quite cold."

Almost as though he had forgotten their respective roles in life, he took her closer under his arm.

She should not have allowed it, but she savored the warmth that radiated from his body. "Ladies' formal attire does not allow for as many layers as men's," she sniffed. "You, at least, have a coat."

"Don't sound so dour, Miss Sedgwyck," said the duke cheerfully. "I see the taproom is still well lit and it will be warm."

Once inside, Lord Malliston still seemed reluctant to part from her. They did not merit so much as a second glance from any of the other patrons, who at this time of night were of greatly varying but generally sedate types. Some were older folks who were, perhaps, lonely and used the inn as a community space, and there were even a few women, while others were men around Lord Malliston's age.

Clerks, she thought, *or perhaps merchants.*

"Do you not wish to retire, my lord?" asked Caroline.

"Of course," he nodded. "Let me show you upstairs."

"I am sure it won't be necessary," she said, less fearful of what anyone might think and more nervous about her own urges and potential lack of self-control. "I can find my own room, again. I did not have *so much* punch," she added with a half-smile. "I am not at all addled."

From that, she silently amended.

Truthfully, the duke's constant proximity all evening had left her stymied.

He was not cloyingly attentive, but he had monopolized her attention, a situation for which she was grateful. She would never say so, but she had been rather frightened of all the guests in their fine clothes. Even the ballroom itself was intimidating, from its glittering candlesticks and chandelier to its exquisite paintings. The Thornlands was grand, but it was not crammed with a lifetime's worth of possessions the way the Poppleton residence was. Lord Malliston seemed to curate his belongings a little more carefully.

"I would never presume to call you *addled*, Miss Sedgwyck," said Lord Malliston. "I am merely being polite."

She sighed. "Very well, my lord. It is at the top of the building, an attic room. I've no complaints at all and it is clean and charming. I expect it was given to me because of my size. But I wonder whether you will even be able to fit in the uppermost stairwell."

He chuckled at her candor. She was so tired that she could not keep it as managed as she would have preferred.

"Let us see whether my stature shall put an end to my chivalry."

Up they went, Caroline being careful not to let the delicate hem of her beautiful dress catch on the wooden steps. By the time they reached the final stretch of stairs, it was clear that Lord Malliston had to compress himself to fit.

She suppressed a giggle.

But when he snorted with amusement, it gave her the courage to say, "My lord, you bring to mind a large cat determined to fit somewhere it cannot."

"It is not an inaccurate comparison," he grumbled.

He stepped aside as much as he could on the narrow landing and she withdrew her key from her little reticule.

Taking a step toward the door, she arched an eyebrow at him and said, "You have accomplished your task. I am safely to my room."

They were unbearably close and the small expanse they shared seemed thick with heat between them. It was equally pleasurable and disarming.

He seemed to feel this way, too, because he neither took a step back to the top stair nor moved any closer to her. He did stare at her mouth more than he stared into her eyes.

I won't kiss you, Lord Malliston, but if you were to kiss me, I would not stop you, she thought desperately.

"So I have," he said, his voice gone husky and soft. "Sleep well,

Miss Sedgwyck."

And before she could register what was happening, he planted a soft, very fleeting kiss to her forehead.

Then he turned, and went carefully but quickly down the stairs.

Chapter Eleven

NATURALLY, SOPHIE AND Phoebe wanted to hear all about the ball, and their interest hardly waned for a fortnight. Although Reeve would have been impatient with them only a month or two ago, he now found their enthusiasm very endearing. Miss Sedgwyck was accommodating of their repetitive questions, and only he noticed the subtle variations in her retellings.

He suspected that she created the minute differences for her own amusement. For example, one day Lady Alderton's dress dripped with beautiful pearls, but when Phoebe asked the next day about the dress, the lady in question's lovely garment was encrusted with the finest diamonds.

Phoebe, having forgotten what Miss Sedgwyck had said about pearls at the utterance of "diamonds", gasped with delight.

Reeve never tired of hearing Miss Sedgwyck paint vivid pictures of the night, even if those verbal paintings never quite matched each other. One drizzling afternoon, while she indulged his daughters yet another time and told them about Lady Anne's nosy questions, he found himself mesmerized by the movement of her lips as she spoke animatedly.

Her words also amused him. She was not straying from the truth at all and, evidently, Lady Anne had been deeply incensed that she could not gather more information from the strange young lady who had accompanied the Duke of Nidderdale.

His girls, however, were fixated on a much different matter.

"Did Papa kiss your hand after the dance, Miss Caroline?" Sophie asked.

It was as though she had not retained anything Miss Sedgwyck had said for the last ten minutes. He could tell by Sophie's expression that she had been dying to ask.

It was a new question, and Reeve saw that Miss Sedgwyck was as stricken as he was. Her fetching eyes widened but, to her credit, she did not appear overly nervous.

"He did not, Sophie," she replied.

Now, she was avoiding his eyes and looking squarely at the girls. Even Phoebe, who was still a little too young to understand how ladies and gentlemen navigated a ball with decorum, was gazing curiously at Miss Sedgwyck.

Reeve thought, *It would hardly be improper to kiss a woman's hand at a ball.*

But he recalled the quick kiss he left on Miss Sedgwyck's forehead, as though he'd been possessed, and blinked.

"Why not?" Sophie persisted. "Duckie said it is proper for a gentleman to kiss a lady's hand after a dance."

"Duckie is correct, Sophie," he said, intervening before Miss Sedgwyck could demure again. "Papa has not been to a dance for a long time, and he did not kiss Miss Caroline's hand. You can be sure that, next time, he will not forget himself."

The children appeared satisfied with his answer. They looked at each other, then at him.

Sophie nodded.

"Good, Papa," she said.

Miss Sedgwyck murmured, "If you will excuse me for a moment, girls..."

Reeve looked over to see that her face was crimson. He caught the hue of her skin just as she nearly flew from the room. It nearly matched her hair. She must have been thinking back to the kind of kiss he had given her.

He was not quite prepared for what Phoebe said next, but was immensely thankful that Miss Sedgwyck was not present to hear it.

"Will you ask Miss Caroline to marry you?"

Sophie vigorously nodded her support, smiling brightly at their father.

"Ah... Phoebe, do you want me to?"

He kept his countenance neutral enough.

"Why, of course she does, yes!" said Sophie, just as Phoebe opened her mouth to respond.

While that propensity for speaking quickly, before she could, had often perturbed the little one, Phoebe just cocked her head at her sister and nodded.

"But am I correct in understanding that you wish it, too, Sophie?" asked Reeve.

Sophie spared him a look that suggested he was a fool for asking. Reeve fell quiet, glancing from her to Phoebe, almost lost in thought.

He knew that as far as they were concerned, their consent sufficiently settled the question.

In the days that followed this abrupt conversation, Reeve continued to dwell on the idea of marrying Miss Sedgwyck. It was hardly the most bizarre idea he had ever entertained in a lifetime of having them.

Sitting in the quiet solitude of his library, Reeve stared out of the window at treetops swaying in the wind. As was his recent habit, he was sipping tea rather than a stronger drink, and his large hand curled around the dainty, warm cup.

Reeve, you're in love with her – you do realize that, don't you, old man?

At least he admitted it to himself, now.

And perhaps it was a foolish man's hope, but he fancied that she reciprocated. On occasion, there would be warmth in one of her glances, a fire in the depths of her eyes that only he could discern. He did not believe that she was impartial to him. Now that they had become friends, they spent more time than ever in each other's company. Everything and everyone in The Thornlands had changed since her arrival, and this included his regard for her.

He thought back to the first afternoon they had ever met, and winced. How cold and cynical he had been.

Ever since Phoebe had asked him her fateful, innocent, insightful question, he found himself constantly wishing he could easily and openly declare his affections for Miss Sedgwyck. It was incredibly heady and disconcerting because he had always been guarded with his emotions. His father had seen to that, even though Reeve's natural temperament always flowed in the vein of poetry and improvisation. He'd merely learned to *act* like less of a poet.

Reeve scowled and sipped some of his tea. Apart from his embarrassment at being in love and his seeming inability to express either sentiment – love, or consternation – there were admittedly several practical obstacles in his way.

For one, he was older than she was. On its own, that was not out of the ordinary, as so many women married older men. Some married men who were old enough to be their fathers. In the end, he was only a decade or so older than Miss Sedgwyck. Possibly a little more than that.

He did not even care that she was a "nobody". He had money and status enough for both of them.

More crucially, he was battle-scarred and nearly deaf. She deserved someone whole, someone whose body and mind had not been torn apart by war and conflict. He wondered what he could give her apart from material comfort and security.

Was he too shaken, too broken, to enter a real love match? In his heart, he had always wanted one. If he was to be painfully frank, he was disappointed and bitter that he'd never had it.

You can offer her more than a comfortable existence, thought Reeve, surprising himself. *You have two beautiful, bright daughters, and you're trying to be better. A better man.*

He recollected all the times he thought he had seen some of his own desire mirrored in her intelligent, graceful face. He chuckled in the empty room.

Even back when she had caught him in the garden with a trollop, she could not completely hide her avid interest under moral indignation.

Not that he was under the impression that Miss Sedgwyck only wanted his body.

Oh, no... he felt that she might wish for the same conclusion to their relationship that he did.

She would be happy to receive you.

But because Reeve could not be sure of this, he continued to shy away from broaching the subject with her.

So their gazes would meet above the table at breakfast, or less frequently, because she was busy during Sophie and Phoebe's lessons. He still believed, or dreamed, that he saw the same questions and ideas within her expression that loomed in his own head. But she would blink and avert her eyes, and the moment of hot clarity would be gone. He would be back to chasing his own tail.

The few times he left The Thornlands to oversee his estate and business affairs, he missed her terribly. None of his journeys were nearly as long as they had been before she declared that he spent too much time away from his family, but they felt longer than anything he had endured.

Ultimately, the decision of whether or not he should confess his feelings was taken out of his hands.

ONE WINDY FRIDAY afternoon in early October, a messenger arrived at

The Thornlands with a letter. The weather was mercurial and awful, and everyone was confined indoors. Lessons were over for the day and Caroline was about to return upstairs to take a leisurely bath when the duke asked that she see him in the library.

Once she arrived, he wordlessly handed her the two pages that had been addressed to Lord Malliston, Duke of Nidderdale.

With a deep sense of foreboding, Caroline said, "My lord, you do not generally have me read your post."

He smiled, but only just.

She dropped her eyes back to the paper and read.

The duke was called by England's Prussian allies to battle. This was merited by the very high recommendation of the Duke of Wellington, whose personal note accompanied the call to arms. It was an irregular summons and Lord Malliston was to be one of a very small number of Englishmen.

Suddenly, Caroline felt as though there were little, live animals fighting in her stomach. She kept reading.

Lord Malliston would be consulting on some aspects of strategy, a move that would ostensibly remove him from harm's way and, importantly, enormous amounts of noise, while engaging his tactical acumen.

He was to report in barely nine days.

Heedless of how little sense the question made, Caroline could only think to ask, "Do you even speak any of the languages of your new commanders?"

He had to smile at how dazed she sounded. "Some. They presumably also speak some English, so we shall muddle along. Besides, maps and colors provide their own language that relies very little on words." He peered at her. "Are you all right?"

"Yes, my lord."

"Good, because I am not certain I feel quite well."

"The girls will be so devastated," she said forlornly. She was afraid to voice her own personal dismay at the turn of events. Caroline longed to beg him not to go but felt it was useless.

She had determined long ago that Lord Malliston was bitter for being sent home from Salamanca only days before an official English victory. Somehow, he felt that this had cheated him of being part of it.

Even if the seal of the Duke of Wellington had not been staring up at him from one of the pages she held in her trembling hands, the duke would not pass up the chance to prove his worthiness. *It's a matter of honor to him*, she thought.

"I want us to tell them together. I think that would help soften the blow," said Lord Malliston, nodding, "but I have something else to say to you."

Overwhelmed by the intensity of her reaction to the summons, Caroline swallowed and returned it to the top of his desk, leaving the Duke of Wellington's note visible. She could not quite bear to see the order itself.

Lord Malliston did not speak for over a minute, and she began to think he was as shocked as she was.

"Shall I fetch some water?" she asked. "Brandy, perhaps?"

"No. I am in love with you, Miss Sedgwyck."

Caroline thought perhaps she had heard him wrong.

Just because you've wanted to hear it does not mean he is saying it.

She had spent hours sternly telling herself that her infatuation with Lord Malliston was neither healthy nor respectful. Why was it that after one and twenty years on this earth without any silly notions about *any* man, *he* turned her head?

His expression, however, was earnest.

She peeked at him and brought a hand to her mouth. "I – I do not understand," she said, barely remembering to speak as loudly as she should.

In truth, she didn't.

"It is extremely selfish of me to put you in this position, now," he said. "But please know, I have been in love with you for quite some time.

"I don't know when it happened. Then, once I realized it, I did not know how to tell you." He began to pace in short steps on the magnificent rug that cushioned the library floor. "You are young and brilliant... and kind." He looked at her, his eyes both harried and desperate.

She tried to remain calm for his sake.

"On the other hand, I am difficult and battle-worn." Bitterly, he gave a short chuckle, and then brightened enough to say with sincerity, "You have been nothing but a blessing to me from the first day we met, even though I did not necessarily deserve a blessing."

"Thank you, my lord," said Caroline. She could not think of what to say to him, other than that. As soon as it left her lips, it sounded banal.

Yet he continued as though she had not spoken.

"I cannot conceive of a day without you. If you will have me, I will always do right by you." Lord Malliston looked at the papers on his desk as though they were a poisonous snake, coiled and ready to strike if he moved too suddenly. "War is upon me again. While I will not be in the fray this time, I am wise enough now to know that anything can happen. *Anything* happened once, after all." He tore his eyes away from the papers and fixed them upon her. "I would never forgive myself if I left without telling you how I truly felt."

The tears she had been holding in check since she'd read the letter began to fall freely. She had longed to hear him say these things since the night of the ball, at least, and most likely before then, if she was being truthful about it.

Now that he said them, she could only cry.

In a near panic, she thought, *You must say something to him, Caroline!* But she was mute.

Lord Malliston did not look annoyed by her tears. On the contrary, he had stilled and was half-smiling. "I do hope your tears are not evidence of your utter disgust with me. Miss Sedgwyck, my heart aches to hear you say that you feel the same. But if you do not reciprocate, please tell me. I will not fault you."

She shook her head, sniffling. "You ridiculous man. *Caroline.* If you are in love with me, you cannot continue calling me *Miss Sedgwyck* for the rest of our lives."

He grinned at her and it was a beautiful sight.

She went to him; his nervous pacing had brought him nearer to the ornate fireplace.

"I love you, Lord Malliston." She took both of his hands in hers, stroking his palms. "I would wait for you even if you decided you were somehow going to the moon."

He watched the movement of her slender fingers on his hands. "Reeve, Caroline. My name is Reeve."

Then, at long last, he kissed her fully and warmly on the lips.

THEY WERE MARRIED within the week, well before nine days had passed. It took some hurried arrangements with the parish and a special dispensation, but due to his standing, Lord Malliston managed to push everything through without difficulty.

Sophie and Phoebe took the news of their father returning to the battlefield about as badly as Caroline feared. Sophie went entirely mute, while Phoebe's lower lip trembled as she tried not to cry. But the promise that she was to be their new mother did comfort them somewhat.

At the simple and intimate ceremony, Duckie was all proud smiles, swanning about and saying to every guest who might listen that she had known the duke would marry Caroline all along, as if she personally took credit for the match.

The duke's rather reprehensible but closest friends, two men whom Caroline did not recognize and one she certainly did, the rake who had mistakenly thought she was a lady for hire that night months ago, were there. Surprisingly, they were on their very best behaviors and the rake, a duke called Bellamy Bingham, personally apologized to Caroline for his crass words. Winking, he said he had known all along that Reeve would take her for a wife.

Even her father confessed to Caroline in private that, once or twice after reading her letters, he hoped her affection for the duke might grow from that of mere esteem and friendship to love.

"As irregular and outlandish as it might have been," Arthur had said, "I found myself hoping."

When news of the marriage reached the wider world, those who had been present at Lord Poppleton's ball agreed they saw it coming. Lord Cuff even sent along a contrite note offering his apologies for insulting the then Miss Sedgwyck.

Reeve merely threw it in the fire after reading it once, prompting Caroline to ask why, and when he reluctantly explained his and Cuff's encounter at the ball with more detail than he had before, she just chuckled.

Of course, there was a strong contingent of the public who believed that there was no love in the marriage at all. The new Lady Malliston, they believed, only wanted the duke's money.

She had to be greedy and mad to marry a man who'd almost assuredly killed his first wife.

The surprising thing was, however, that some of the eager gossipers spread the opposite explanation.

It *must* have been a love match since the former Miss Sedgwyck was a commoner and not even a wealthy one. The duke must love her.

Cautiously, the people who favored this line of thought wished only the best for Lady Malliston.

✿❋✿

THE NIGHT FOLLOWING their nuptials, Caroline entered the duke's bedroom as his bride. It was the first time she had ever seen it and she looked around with interest. Like every other room in The Thornlands, it was stately and rather large. The furnishings were all dark, lacquered wood that glowed in the candlelight, and Reeve's bedclothes were blue brocade accented with bronze. Everything had its place and nothing about it was disorderly. A maid had placed a bouquet of roses on the dresser. They must have been hothouse flowers or late garden blooms. Their honeyed scent filled the room, contrasting with the bracing citrus smells of wood polish and Reeve's cologne.

She was not nervous, but she was curious and a little apprehensive. Reeve seemed to sense this, because he gave her space as she surveyed his room and did not rush her to the bed.

"It suits you, in here," she said. "I cannot picture anyone but you in this room."

She was not stalling for time. She merely had little idea of how to initiate what was bound to happen next. All her theoretical knowledge on the subject, which was considerable, apparently deserted her head when she entered Reeve's personal chambers.

She kept a smirk well off her face as she thought back to Aunt Lydia trying to explain *the things* that happened between women and men.

Books, even the obscene books that had left her curious and agitated, proved far more instructive and engaging than her aunt's flustered, hushed nattering about *the things*. And none of Caroline's friends were terribly fast young ladies, but a few of them had engaged in clandestine trysts before marrying. She had learned much, sometimes too much, from their experiences.

His smile was gentle. "I tried to make it as peaceful as possible.

Until you came, it was the eye of the storm." He approached her slowly. "May I?"

Her breath caught a little when he skimmed his fingertips down the back of her dress. It was new, as all of her clothes now would be, and a delicate leaf green satin that set off her eyes and clung to her in a manner she felt was risqué but was obviously appreciated by her husband.

"Play lady's maid, you mean?"

"You *are* Lady Malliston, now," Reeve said. "Someone must until we can find you one."

He pressed a kiss to the base of her neck, and her knees went wobbly as her cheeks warmed. Part of her was amazed at the rapidity of her reactions, and a much larger part wanted him to keep provoking them.

As though her mind was running off in its own direction, heedless of any sense, she blurted out, "After we... after tonight, would you ever... in the garden, with me?"

It was hardly intelligible, and Reeve laughed, but he caught her meaning.

"I thought you were concerned for my – our – daughters' sensibilities. You gave me quite the diatribe." He kissed her neck again and she gave a little, low moan. "But maybe, just maybe, I can arrange for Duckie to go with them into town one afternoon..."

He used his teeth very lightly on her skin and she shivered.

She discovered that his hands were still moving as he spoke, ranging along her back, then sneaking around her torso to fondle her breasts softly. It was intoxicating.

Caroline had never been touched in such a way, but she decided right then that she adored it. She all but melted, leaning back into him. "Reeve..." she murmured.

They retreated to the bed, eventually, but Reeve made a terrible lady's maid.

He only fully undressed her before the second time they took pleasure in each other on that night.

THE DAY BEFORE Reeve was scheduled to depart, Caroline planned a surprise for him. All she said was for him to meet her at half-past ten in the morning at the pianoforte. It was easy to accomplish what she wanted without him realizing. He was busy seeing to his own affairs before he left, and as Lady Malliston, she now had the run of the house and the command of the servants. She was a much better housekeeper than Mrs. Humphrey had ever been, and she took to the running of a large household like a duck to water. It suited her pragmatic mind.

All the surprise took was dispatching Alice to town for some new sheet music. The day of the wedding, she had also spoken to her father, who was very pleased to help her.

Once everything she needed was procured, Caroline instructed her husband to do as she said.

True to his word, he came indoors at half-past ten with a bloom in his olive skin and mussed hair. He smelled of damp leaves and horses. She smiled at him from over the pianoforte.

"Come," she said, motioning to him.

Puzzled, he still kissed her before sitting on the bench to her right. Then he kissed her again, and Caroline found herself almost deliriously distracted. Though pleasurable, that would not do.

"Reeve," she said, a little breathless, but through a laugh. "There will be time for that tonight."

"What's this, then?" He eyed the pianoforte and the crisp, new sheet music warily.

"A gift," she said. "I thought I could play for you before you left. That way you can hum or sing something that you will always associate with me." She kissed the dubious expression from his face.

"Don't look so skeptical. It's only a folk song that I'd forgotten until I started to think of them." With a note of playfulness, she added, "We shall see if it fits the elegant and dignified pianoforte."

"Anything you play with these graceful fingers will fit it." He took her hand and kissed each of her fingertips.

"You cannot dissuade me from my task," she said archly, reclaiming her hands and starting to play.

It was nothing complex and certainly nothing particularly aristocratic. She doubted that most of the folks who had known it over the years had sheet music for any instrument to accompany them.

An old song about a squire falling in love with someone above his station, it was one of Father's favorites and she had dim memories of him teaching it to her when she was very little.

The shopkeeper in town, she was told, took a few hours to find or transcribe the music she requested. Reeve did not know it yet, but there were two songs she had in store for him. This one posed the larger challenge for the shopkeeper. She wondered if the man had simply fabricated something for her to play.

She would ask Alice and be sure to send along some extra coin for him if that was the case.

If I had Father's talent, she thought, *I could just make up an accompaniment.*

Without further delay, she sang the words confidently even if her fingers still faltered a little on the pianoforte. The song had a happy ending and, although there were several hurdles in the tale and there were different variations on the same verses, the squire was always able to marry his lady despite time, station, and distance separating them temporarily.

Reeve seemed transfixed, for his eyes never left her face once as she sang.

Even when she finished, he gazed at her for some time before talking. "Did Arthur teach you that?"

"Of course he did."

"He must like it. I hadn't heard it until he sang it for us. I expect on account of my comparatively sheltered upbringing," he added with a lopsided smile.

Caroline chuckled. "It is not a lewd song," she said. "But I don't imagine your own music tutor would have used it for you to practice."

"No, he did not," said Reeve, musing. "He was a hard taskmaster. He only chose the most difficult runs and airs. I was lucky to be naturally talented."

"Would you like to know a secret, my lord?"

"Only if you do not call me that ever again."

Lightly, she cuffed him on the shoulder. "It is not an easy habit to break."

"I'll see it broken sooner or later, Lady Malliston."

She glowed at the warmth in "Lady Malliston" and noted to herself that he never sounded as taken when he used it to refer to her tragic predecessor. "Well, I am glad you liked it, but I chose it for its simplicity. I am no musician. I pray any children we have together take after *you* in that regard."

The words left her as naturally as an expelled breath, but they fell quiet and regarded each other. Until her unexpected and unconventional marriage, Caroline had not given much thought to having children of her own. She trusted that if it was meant to be, it would happen. Now, the possibility was both very welcome and acutely new to her.

"I did not just *like* it," said Reeve. "I loved it. It's a comforting story, is it not?" He smiled at her. "And a romantic one."

"I thought so."

"And, to be clear, I will adore any of our children no matter what their particular aptitudes turn out to be." He stroked her thigh through her dress, the old fawn one she had arrived in. She did not have enough new clothing to constitute a whole wardrobe, yet. "I hope they all will have their mother's bracing good sense, even if it means their opinions may be rather quickly voiced."

She laughed with delight and asked, "Tell me, you did not think my directness wicked, did you?"

He pretended to consider her question until she scowled.

"I found it incredibly jarring, especially coming from such a delicate woman. Never wicked or wrong."

"But endearing?"

"We *did* end up married."

Caroline leaned in and kissed him, teasing his lips gently with her tongue until they parted and he groaned.

She said, with their faces close together, "And so we did. But at first, if anyone had asked me what was more likely—were you going to be my future husband, or would I suddenly sprout wings and fly away—I would have said the latter."

He brought his ruined hand to her cheek.

"Was I so repugnant to you?"

"No, Reeve. You were formidable in the same way, oh… a mountain is, but you only ever repulsed me when you left Phoebe and Sophie open to potential danger or corruption," she said, turning her head to kiss his palm. "I sensed or wanted to have faith that you were a better man than you appeared. And before I even thought about that, well, I now have no problem telling you that I thought about doing very *wifely* things with you."

Her confession garnered a wolfish smirk. Reeve pushed his hair back and it seemed like he was recalling past scenes in their acquaintance. "I *wondered* if you did, although naturally I would never have asked," he said with a measure of guilt that still did not dwarf the satisfaction in his eyes.

"Naturally," she said primly.

Then she deliberated internally, for the second component to her wedding gift might not be something he enjoyed so happily. She took another sheaf of music from the compartment under the bench and spread it before them. This song was new to her, and she had especially selected it with a little advice from her father.

Reeve studied it, then her face.

"What is this?"

"The second part of your gift," she said.

Nervously, she began to play with just her left hand. It was not her dominant one, but the song was pretty and simple enough that even she could manage. She took her eyes away from the music and glanced at him invitingly, lovingly.

Reeve watched her fingers until comprehension dawned in his eyes.

"You are kind, but I don't know if this is advisable." He shook his head slowly.

Caroline was not fully surprised. She halted her playing and said gently, "We could play together."

"I cannot play at all, my love," he insisted.

"You can," she said.

"Not the way I'd like," he confessed.

"That's why it is a gift," she explained. "We can make music together, you see? We can share it, and you can think on it in the darker times." She pushed too specific of an idea of what "darker times" might mean for Reeve from her mind.

War is never without *them*, she thought.

"What a lovely gift!"

Phoebe chose that instant to trundle into the room, having outpaced both her sister and Duckie, who was minding the girls for Caroline. Evidently, she had lingered long enough in the doorway to understand what was going on. She carried a bundle of colorful autumn flowers and tracked in a trail of leaves, some of which were embedded in her hair. Though she presented a small mess, Caroline was secretly pleased she arrived when she did.

"Do you think so, Phoebe?" asked Caroline. "I thought so, as well."

Phoebe went up to her father's side of the bench and nodded as seriously as a magistrate. "You miss playing, Papa," she said, clearly and with pronounced volume. "This is a new way to play. It doesn't mean it is worse than how you played before."

Unable to counter that, for it was sensible, Reeve said, "When did you become so wise, little one?"

Phoebe shrugged and stuck a small pink rose into his lapel.

Sophie caught up to her shortly, puffing as she joined Phoebe's side. "Duckie told me to tell you that there are biscuits in the kitchen." She looked at Reeve, then Caroline, curiously. "Why are both of you on the bench?"

"Miss Caroline, I mean, Caroline, is trying to get Papa to play," said Phoebe.

"How can he play with his hand?"

"Well, Sophie, I thought that we could play a song together," Caroline said.

Rather shamelessly, Caroline was using her new daughters in the same way Reeve had once used them to coax her into staying on at The Thornlands.

Sophie saw at once that Reeve was the problem. She grabbed his injured hand and clung to it. "Papa, do play! It would make you happy. I just know it."

Reeve looked from one small eager face to the other. He worried his bottom lip.

I don't know if he's more embarrassed or eager, thought Caroline. He missed playing so very much that his inclination toward pride might be losing against his desire to make music, again.

"You could be right, Sophie," said Reeve. With resignation, he glanced at Caroline, who tried not to look too openly pleased at his capitulation. "Very well, Wife. I see that there are no lyrics to this song. Only notes." He positioned his right hand so that his fingers grazed the keys. "That is just as well, for I am dreadfully out of practice and both singing *and* playing would be beyond me. Do proceed."

Her heart feeling bright, she began to play.

When he joined in, the manor itself seemed to mirror their smiles. They were both tenuous at first, but soon Reeve gained more verve and his playing grew in intensity. Had he not been so attuned to keeping her pace, he would have shown her up entirely. She could see what sort of musician he had been before Salamanca, and had a far better understanding and a much deeper sympathy for his loss when he realized he could not play as he was accustomed to doing his whole life.

But together, thought Caroline, *we can make a whole.*

Epilogue

T HE DAYS WHILE Reeve was away were long. Nights, though, were longer and more excruciating. Caroline was convinced that time had conspired against her to occupy more of itself and drive her mad.

She could no longer deny that she missed her husband so sorely that each time she actually thought about how much she missed him, she could not breathe.

Each day since he had left was a battle. Her own battle. She endeavored to be brave and soothing especially for Sophie and Phoebe, but her abilities were growing taxed.

She supervised the servants, taught her daughters, and conversed with Duckie and Edgar whenever she could. In this manner, her days were filled with activities that drove longing to the recesses of her mind, but she felt the house was haunted by Reeve's absence. He was everywhere, yet nowhere.

She once heard Sophie sagely caution Phoebe not to mention Papa in Caroline's hearing. This made her feel almost painfully guilty, because she then knew that she was not keeping up the brave façade.

The nights were unbearable. She slept in his bed, first because it smelled of him, then simply because it was his. It was the only place where she allowed herself to cry and if anyone overheard her, they did not mention it. Sometimes, she would frequent his library, that sanctum he so loved, and doze off on one of the sofas or armchairs. It was merely a half-sleep and she was caught between wakefulness and slumber. Her dreams were torturous because they were always carnal, always of him, and he always evaporated when she opened her eyes.

Recently, she had also taken to sleeping, if she could even fall into slumber, with her hands curved protectively over her stomach. It was not something she did quite consciously. She would simply realize, at some point, that she had folded her hands across her belly. No one knew of her condition. She had only discovered she was with child a week past, and although she didn't know when Reeve would return, she wanted him to be the first to know about it.

She hid her ghastly morning nausea and the inevitable fatigue with a soldier's fortitude. Pregnancy could have gone either way for her, she surmised, and of course her mother could not advise her. With the help of an apothecary in town, she learned what teas she could brew to ease some of her symptoms and this helped her maintain the illusion that nothing had changed.

Then the news of victory at Leipzig circulated like wildfire across the whole of England.

There were also reports of the many lives lost. It had been a fearsome, bloody battle with very heavy casualties on both sides.

The Thornlands anxiously awaited news of their duke. Caroline tried with all her might to keep the girls engaged and distracted, but her own nerves made it all the more difficult.

In turn, Duckie did all she could to alleviate some of Caroline's anxieties, but she, like everyone else in the household, knew that only Lord Malliston's safe return would remedy Caroline's pitiable state.

Relief came one dark night.

All was silent and everyone had gone to bed except for Caroline. Sleep was entirely beyond her that evening, so she was roaming the halls like a voiceless banshee or tragic specter as tears trailed down her cheeks.

You are being ridiculous, she thought. But for some reason known only to her and her unborn child, she would cry at the drop of a hat in a way she never had before.

She thought she imagined the sound of the carriage.

Pregnancy, she had discovered in even her short experience, was havoc on her senses. Her sense of smell seemed heightened to a preternatural degree, she was always hungry but could hardly eat for feeling ill, and even her hearing had apparently improved.

But she also sometimes heard things that were not there. Perhaps that was not the unborn babe, but the distress that she herself was in.

She stilled, waiting, squinting out of one of the large windows on the ground floor.

She heard it again. It was not her imagination. Eyes wide and with a hand clasped against her mouth, Caroline carefully ran to Edgar's room in the dark and roused him from his deep slumber. She didn't care how unseemly or addled she might seem entering his room in her slippers, nightdress, and pelisse.

"Lord Malliston is coming, Edgar," she insisted.

I refuse to believe it is anyone else or a bearer of horrible news.

Caroline could tell that Edgar was trying to assess if she was having a turn or had gone mad like the former Lady Malliston. Still, the consummate butler, he went into action.

He woke Alice, Duckie, a stable boy, and the duke's valet, and told them to keep watch at the massive front door. Yawning, he stood with them.

Scarcely a minute after they had gathered, they, too, heard the unmistakable sounds of wheels.

Caroline wanted to shout, *"You see?"* Ultimately, however, she restrained herself.

It was not long before the unmarked carriage, pulled by unfamiliar dun horses, came into full view. It was barely illuminated by their candles, but the night was clear and the full moon cast some light on the scene.

Although Edgar and the others protested, Caroline rushed to the carriage just as it came to a halt. She had to see who it contained and could not stand to wait a moment longer. Dreadful visions of the worst flashed before her mind's eye, but she tried not to heed them.

Then Reeve flew from the compartment without waiting for the driver or a footman to help him.

Behind her, she heard Edgar say, "Good Lord, Alice, do go and wake the girls." She did not bother to look at him or nod. Phoebe and Sophie would never forgive anybody if they did not wake them the very instant that Papa returned. Alice must have shuffled off immediately to do so, for there was the sound of quick footsteps in the dirt, then of the massive front door opening.

Reeve was haggard and his dark hair had grown longer and more unkempt, but he was sound. Mutely, Caroline just stared at him, finding that, for all her restless energy, she was rooted to the spot.

He flashed her a brilliant smile, then gathered her to him.

"I am never parting from you," said Caroline, her words muffled against his chest. "If you are ever summoned to battle, again, I shall stow away in whatever conveyance you're taking and dress as a man to stay by your side."

She felt, rather than heard, his joyful laughter. "I cannot make out a word you are saying, dear heart."

Caroline pulled away from him enough to look into his face. "What do you mean?"

Still smiling, Reeve tapped his ear for emphasis. "My apologies, but you'll have to speak up for this old man."

"Oh. Oh! Of course," said Caroline. *How can I have forgotten?* "I said, I am never parting from you, and if you are ever summoned to battle again, you shall have to monitor your conveyances for a stowaway."

"Was there something else about you dressing as a man? Or was that just wishful thinking? I believe you'd look quite fetching in trousers," he said roguishly, perhaps to quell the tears that streamed down her face.

She laughed and pushed him a little against his collarbone. *"Reeve."*

As the stable boy was conferring with the carriage driver and the carriage rumbled past the two of them, Reeve grew more somber.

"I thought of you every day while I was gone," he said. "Always."

"Was it awful?"

Caroline was naturally too curious for her own good. As soon as she asked, she wished she had not, both for his peace of mind and her own comfort. Of course it had been awful. She knew that for Reeve, the supposed glamor of being a favorite of the Duke of Wellington had worn off as soon as shrapnel stole his fingers and the bulk of his hearing.

"Not as awful as Salamanca for me. Not in the way that you imagine," said Reeve after a breath. He stroked her hair. "But you had everything to do with that, Caroline. You were my North Star in the long, dark night of war. And my longing for you was unbearable at times."

Surreptitiously, she watched for any telling winces as she stroked his back.

Has he been injured? It would be typical of him to pretend he has not, even if he has.

"I missed you," she said. "I fear I was not so bright in your absence as you imagined me to be."

"I might be concerned if you had been happier," said Reeve, brushing away some of her tears with the pad of his thumb. "But it is done, and I am here with no fewer fingers and no less hearing than before."

"Don't be glib," she admonished him. But she gave a little chuckle all the same.

"I am not. I'm merely counting my blessings."

"We spoke about you each day," she said. "The girls and I." She smiled fondly through her tears. "Suddenly, many more of our history lessons had to do with military tacticians. It helped them, you know. Trying to understand what your life was like. They are far more inquisitive than you've given them credit for. I think we have two new bluestockings on our hands."

Sophie had developed an avid interest in the ancient worlds of Rome, Egypt, and Greece, while Phoebe was endlessly fascinated by, of all figures, the infamous Cardinal Richelieu. Putting their father's career in context with what had come before appeared to allay their more pressing fears. Not everyone died in battle.

It did not stop them from missing him. Continuing, she said as much. "They wished for your return just as much as I did."

While they'd always missed Papa before, this seemed to be different and Caroline knew why. For the first time in their very young lives, the girls felt that Reeve truly loved and valued them. They no longer had to wonder if they were inconvenient burdens, because he had endeavored well before his departure to demonstrate their importance to him.

He'd left an even bigger void in their world than he had before because he was more tangibly and lovingly part of it.

"I wanted nothing more than to come home to all of you."

"And you did," said Caroline.

Reeve glanced around them. "Where are the beautiful little creatures? This is all lovely, but suspiciously serene."

"They were abed. Edgar sent Alice to rouse them as soon as he knew it was you."

"Were you asleep, too?"

"No," admitted Caroline. "I have found it inordinately difficult since you left."

For more than one reason, she thought. *Little one, you have kept me up more than I thought was possible.*

It was far too early in her pregnancy for her to show, and Reeve had no notion that he was holding both his wife *and* future child in his arms.

"Papa!"

Shrill, happy, ecstatic shrieks came from the steps as both of the girls came sprinting to them.

Caroline turned slightly and saw that Alice had all but given up trying to keep Phoebe or Sophie in hand. The girls ran on their little legs, still clothed only in their nightrails, slippers, and shawls. They must have seen their Papa through the windows.

She smiled her thanks at the maid and realized approvingly that several lights were now lit in the manor. Duckie and the duke's valet had both disappeared, as had Edgar. They were readying things as best they could for Lord Malliston's abrupt return.

No one would be going back to bed for some time tonight. There was too much joy in the air. Caroline would be completely unable to make either Phoebe, who usually could tire easily, or Sophie, go back to sleep especially if they knew the adults were still awake. Nor would she want to impose such a thing upon them. This was too special a night.

Reeve scooped Phoebe up in his arms as Sophie, who felt herself much too dignified for that in her advanced age, tugged at his dirty trousers.

"Papa," Sophie said. "We did not know you would be home tonight."

Meanwhile, Phoebe goggled at Reeve as though he was an apparition.

"Neither did I, my sweet," he said. "They stuck me in a carriage and off I went."

"I missed you," said Phoebe firmly.

Mirroring her seriousness, Reeve said, "And I, you, little one."

"Will you have to leave again?" Sophie demanded.

"No," said Reeve. "We are staying together. I shall simply refuse to leave my wonderful family, no matter who sends me a summons."

Caroline couldn't manage to keep her secret to herself, at that.

It was all too surreal and beautiful out here under the stars. As though Heaven itself was pleased at this turn of events, the sky was clear and looked down upon them. The girls. Reeve.

"Our *growing* family." Caroline made sure she spoke in a tenor that Reeve could hear.

She was rewarded by his look of pure surprise as he nearly dropped little Phoebe, but he recovered his poise enough to eke out, "Truly?"

Then his surprise was supplanted by utter delight. Caroline nodded in affirmation.

"How long?" he asked, almost dreamily.

"As you see," she said wryly, but with pleasure, gesturing at herself, "not very long. But long enough to know for certain."

"To know *what* for certain?"

Sophie was completely mystified. For her, her parents might as well have been speaking Spanish or German. But she could sense that the exchange was somehow important.

Smiling, Caroline got on her haunches so that she could be at eye-level with Sophie, careless of the dirt. "You and Phoebe are going to have a little brother or sister."

Sophie said prosaically, "Well, I already know how to take care of Phoebe. I don't see how I would be bad at taking care of another sibling."

Caroline bit back a laugh at her forthright response.

"Oh!" exclaimed Phoebe from her perch in Reeve's arms. "I shan't be the baby, now."

Caroline waited to see if this was a good or bad pronouncement. She wanted the girls to be happy, but also understood it was a massive change for all of them and did not expect it to be easily digested by her daughters.

Reeve appeared to share Caroline's thoughts, for although he looked radiantly pleased, he said neutrally, "No, darling."

But Phoebe giggled and said, "I didn't want to be the youngest forever."

Relief written on his careworn, exhausted face, Reeve said, "Then you have your wish." He kissed the top of her head. After sharing a long, happy look with Caroline, he suggested, "Well, perhaps we should all head indoors? It *is* the middle of the night. And I've received the happiest news I could have... so I feel a drink may be in order. Or celebratory biscuits and hot chocolate for those young ladies who cannot yet partake in strong drinks." He winked at Sophie and Phoebe.

Caroline rose and took his left hand. "It seems we have a new life to begin together."

Shifting Phoebe in his grasp, Reeve bent down and kissed Caroline softly. It was a promise of the sweet things to come. "I can hear the pianoforte calling, too."

About the Author

Whitney is a bit of a wanderer and something of a bluestocking. She's been telling stories since childhood, when she would rewrite the endings of her favorite books and movies (or add "deleted scenes" to them). When she's not writing or reading, she enjoys cooking, dancing, and going for long walks with no specific destination in mind.

Made in the USA
San Bernardino, CA
18 August 2019